Donated to
**SAINT PAUL PUBLIC LIBRARY**

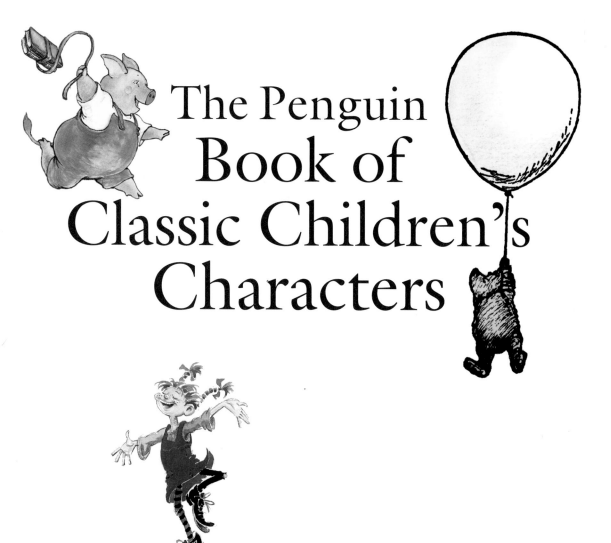

# The Penguin
## Book of
## Classic Children's
## Characters

Dutton Children's Books • Lodestar Books • Frederick Warne & Co. • Viking
NEW YORK

# Contents

# Introduction

Babies beguiled by the sight of other babies soon become children eager for stories whose characters hold up further reflections of themselves.

The young see characters everywhere: in the lone pea left on a dinner plate; in the box of buttons taken down for sorting on a rainy afternoon. Dolls, action figures, and games from patty-cake to Pac-Man extend the lists of characters to be tried on, lived with, and one day put aside. The luckiest children are those who first experience storybooks, and the characters to be met in them, not as required reading in school but as natural additions to the active fantasy lives they lead anyway.

Some stories piggyback on this childhood fascination with things coming to life. Winnie-the-Pooh in his wood, Corduroy lost and found in a vast and puzzling store, take their cue from the wish that favorite toys might one day become full-fledged companions.

The strong connection children feel with the animal world underlies their devotion to a wide variety of favorite characters. The sly wit of *The Tale of Peter Rabbit* builds on the knowledge that bunnies and children have much in common when curiosity lands them in thickets of trouble. The humor of *The Story of Ferdinand,* on the other hand, arises in part from obvious differences between animals and humans: while some children might act like Ferdinand, no real bull ever would.

The sheer *otherness* of animals makes them useful at times as story characters meant to pinpoint human folly from a safe and clarifying distance. Children wish to be taken seriously, and as they, like David McPhail's Pig Pig, come to associate work with the "real world" of their elders, their own toys and games may begin to seem small. Caught up in this childhood predicament, Pig Pig turns in desperation to his mother, whose wise and canny words of advice help him to channel shapeless longings into a real job that is just his size.

There generally comes a time when children would rather read about people than pigs. Like Pig Pig, the young narrator of Barbara

Cooney's semi-autobiographical *Miss Rumphius* has yet to accomplish much in the worldly sense: she is still a child. What she has done, however, is recognize in her great-aunt's example a life worthy of emulation.

Literature makes heroes of those who learn from experience and fools of those who lack the curiosity or the wit to do so. Curiosity, a spirit of enterprise, and a strong sense of right and wrong prompt ten-year-old Encyclopedia Brown to become "America's Sherlock Holmes in sneakers." Doubtless also inspired by the example of his father, who earns his living as the local chief of police, Encyclopedia has a private agreement with his dad. Whenever an especially difficult case comes before Idaville's chief of police, Encyclopedia solves it.

Children also know better than their elders in Robert McCloskey's classic tales of Centerburg, U.S.A. All-American Homer Price enjoys tinkering with mechanical gadgetry. But when a dough-nut-making machine will not shut off, Homer cannot help wondering, as the stacks of unwanted sinkers multiply, whether the modern "labor saving devices" are worth the trouble.

The need to know thickens the plot of heroes' lives, often prompting them to rebel against whatever authority would try to limit their freedom to experience life. Madeline simply must break ranks with her schoolmates as they march "in two straight lines" through the streets of Paris. We love this little girl all the more for being the smallest in her group; she is the most vulnerable as well as the bravest. We love Peter Rabbit for venturing forth—against his mother's wishes!—into Mr. McGregor's garden, unable to resist the temptation to do the bold, creative, forbidden thing.

Well-behaved characters rarely hold readers' attention for long: who cares how Peter Rabbit's obedient sisters spent *their* day? Still, the model children met in stories do serve a useful purpose from the young reader's point of view. All children harbor a longing for order and a need for rules. Creativity, which presupposes a certain tolerance for disorder, probably cannot sustain itself without a counterbalancing sense that even chaos has its limits. Young readers may thrill to imagine themselves as Peter or Madeline or Pippi Longstocking while at the same time realizing that they are actually more like the supporting characters—for instance, *Pippi Longstocking*'s Annika and Tommy, who are happy to return home to their parents at the end of the day.

At age nine, Pippi Longstocking has all the strength of a force of nature, all the money she will ever need, a horse, a house, and happiness. Nothing is beyond her reach—except growing up, and under the circumstances that can hardly matter to her.

In contrast to Pippi, characters like Sam Gribley, the hero of Jean Craighead George's *My Side of the Mountain,* immerse themselves in a struggle for independence from the constraints typically imposed on children by family life and by childhood itself. That struggle *is* Sam's story. In the high-stakes form of rebellion chosen by him, running away from home becomes a headlong running *toward* a more grown-up kind of self-acceptance and self-knowledge.

Probably all children imagine taking off on an adventure like Sam's, and it is certainly heady fun to read about his close shaves and triumphs. It is another thing, however, to risk starvation and death while scrambling to set up housekeeping in the hollow of a tree.

Yet even if, in reality, most children do not run away, they find ways to practice their survival skills just by living in the daily company of imperfect parents and sometimes disagreeable siblings and friends. In *Tales of a Fourth Grade Nothing,* Judy Blume shows that helping to supervise a preschooler's birthday party can seem a fairly hellish experience. It makes all the difference that Peter, the fourth grader who bears the brunt of the little revelers' antics, gets to tell the story in his own words. Action in Judy Blume has as much to do with emotional discharge, the healthy letting off of a little steam, as it does with who licked the roses off the birthday cake and who peed on the carpet. Yet Blume orchestrates Peter's version of events in such a way as to make us recognize the humor in what happened.

The poignancy of Peter's story lies in his having been catapulted into a distant orbit by the arrival in his household of his younger brother, Fudge. Peter will never again occupy the center of the universe, and he knows it.

All children, of course, must make this painful discovery sooner or later—if not during their first years of life at home, then certainly on entering school, where classmates are even more likely than sisters and brothers to jostle for position and toss fairness to the wind. At five and a half, Roald Dahl's Matilda already knows that the world can turn a deaf ear to anyone, however lovable and bright. As the narrator of *Matilda* reports, this particular girl was "a little late" in starting school because "Matilda's parents, who weren't very concerned one way or the other about their daughter's education, had forgotten to make the proper arrangements in advance."

Yet what does the child do on her first day of school but shine, revealing to the first sympathetic teacher she meets an astonishing head for mathematics and literature, and a heart to match.

Matilda can hardly have had a more promising start. Yet not all is well. Matilda's teacher, Miss Honey, is not alone, it turns out, in being aptly named; so too are Crunchem Hall and the head of the school, the loathsome Miss Trunchbull. The really hard lessons Matilda learns will come not from books but from the manner in which her fellow Crunchemites choose to treat her and one another.

Matilda's superhuman intelligence, like Pippi Longstocking's herculean strength, proves more than a match for the small-minded adults who would dampen her spirits. How, though, might an ordinary mortal defend himself against the outrageous caprices of a callous overlord—say, the greedy and barbarous Count of Hamelin-Loring in Lloyd Alexander's *The Marvelous Misadventures of Sebastian*? Faced with this dilemma, Sebastian, a young court musician who stands falsely accused of insulting the Count, goes into involuntary exile, during the course of which all his inner resources will be tested.

As Sebastian sets out, he is less a hero than a victim of circumstance (albeit a charmer), although he *has* managed to save a white cat from the hands of superstitious villagers, who mistook the cat for a witch. Welcoming the battle-scarred animal as his first traveling companion, Sebastian remarks, "If you could talk, as those cowards in Dorn believed, you could surely tell them a few tales." As his own story unfolds, the young innocent's flight turns willy-nilly into a series of heroic adventures.

*Mis*adventures, rather, as Lloyd Alexander pointedly writes. For Alexander, the comic element is intrinsic to any honest account of heroism. Real heroes emerge by fits and starts. They tend to be slow learners. If Sebastian ends up with a bucket on his head, so, now and then, do the best of us. That being the case, we had better be prepared to laugh at ourselves in the mirror.

Matilda, that quick study, knows this as well. When Miss Honey asks her if she thinks that all children's books "ought to have funny bits in them," she replies, "I do. Children are not so serious as grown-ups and they love to laugh."

Here, then, is a book with lots of funny bits, and here is a hall of mirrors.

Leonard S. Marcus
July 1997

# The Penguin
# Book of
# Classic Children's
# Characters

# Corduroy

from *Corduroy* by Don Freeman
**THE VIKING PRESS, 1968**

# About Corduroy

*Corduroy* began with Don Freeman's idea to do a story about a department store in which a character wanders around at night after the doors close. He wanted to show the vast differences between the luxury of a department store and the simple life most of us live. Recalling the birth of *Corduroy,* he said, "I don't know how or when a toy bear came into my life, but he must have come from way out of my past. You know, I could just see a bear wearing corduroy overalls with one button missing . . . the minute I settled on Corduroy and Lisa, everything came together." Although the idea for *Corduroy* came to Mr. Freeman easily, it took him many drafts to perfect the story. But the results were certainly worth it. Children responded so well to *Corduroy* that the book is now a classic and the bear one of the most beloved of all time.

**Don Freeman** (1908–78) was born in San Diego, California, and moved to New York City to study art, making his living as a jazz trumpeter. Coming home on the subway one night, he became so engrossed in sketching his fellow passengers that he accidentally left his trumpet behind. With the loss of his horn, Mr. Freeman turned his talents to art full-time. He worked as a freelance graphic artist covering the New York theater scene, contributing to *The New York Times* and the New York *Herald Tribune*.

Mr. Freeman's venture into children's books came quite unexpectedly. A librarian friend encouraged him to send a story he had written for his son to a publisher. The story was accepted, and he was hooked. He went on to write and illustrate over twenty-five picture books for children, including *Beady Bear, Dandelion, Mop Top, Norman the Doorman, Corduroy,* and the follow-up, *A Pocket for Corduroy*. At the time of his death in 1978, the *Chicago Tribune* said: "Don Freeman was one of those fortunates who could draw and write with the same warm charm and simple directness that a child instantly responds to."

Corduroy is a bear who once lived in the toy department of a big store. Day after day he waited with all the other animals and dolls for somebody to come along and take him home.

The store was always filled with shoppers buying all sorts of things, but no one ever seemed to want a small bear in green overalls.

Then one morning a little girl stopped and looked
straight into Corduroy's bright eyes.
"Oh, Mommy!" she said. "Look! There's the very bear
I've always wanted."
"Not today, dear." Her mother sighed. "I've spent too
much already. Besides, he doesn't look new. He's lost the
button to one of his shoulder straps."

Corduroy watched them sadly as they walked away.

"I didn't know I'd lost a button," he said to himself.
"Tonight I'll go and see if I can find it."

Late that evening, when all the shoppers had gone and
the doors were shut and locked, Corduroy climbed

carefully down from his shelf and began searching everywhere on the floor for his lost button.

Suddenly he felt the floor moving under him! Quite by accident he had stepped onto an escalator—and up he went!

"Could this be a mountain?" he wondered. "I think I've always wanted to climb a mountain."

He stepped off the escalator as it reached the next floor,
and there, before his eyes, was a most amazing sight—

tables and chairs and lamps and sofas, and rows and rows
of beds. "This must be a palace!" Corduroy gasped. "I
guess I've always wanted to live in a palace."

He wandered around admiring the furniture.
"This must be a bed," he said. "I've always wanted to
sleep in a bed." And up he crawled onto a large, thick
mattress.

All at once he saw something small and round.
"Why, here's my button!" he cried. And he tried to pick
it up. But, like all the other buttons on the mattress, it
was tied down tight.

He yanked and pulled with both paws until POP! Off came the button—and off the mattress Corduroy toppled,

*bang* into a tall floor lamp. Over it fell with a crash!

Corduroy didn't know it, but there was someone else awake in the store. The night watchman was going his rounds on the floor above. When he heard the crash he came dashing down the escalator.

"Now who in the world did that!" he exclaimed.
"Somebody must be hiding around here!"

He flashed his light under and over sofas and beds until he came to the biggest bed of all. And there he saw two fuzzy brown ears sticking up from under the cover.

"Hello!" he said. "How did *you* get upstairs?"

The watchman tucked Corduroy under his arm and carried him down the escalator

and set him on the shelf in the toy department with the other animals and dolls.

Corduroy was just waking up when the first customers came into the store in the morning. And there, looking at him with a wide, warm smile, was the same little girl he'd seen only the day before.

"I'm Lisa," she said, "and you're going to be my very own bear. Last night I counted what I've saved in my piggy bank and my mother said I could bring you home."

"Shall I put him in a box for you?" the saleslady asked.
"Oh, no thank you," Lisa answered. And she carried
Corduroy home in her arms.

She ran all the way up four flights of stairs, into her family's apartment, and straight to her own room.

Corduroy blinked. There was a chair and a chest of drawers, and alongside a girl-size bed stood a little bed just the right size for him. The room was small, nothing like that enormous palace in the department store. "This must be home," he said. "I *know* I've always wanted a home!"

Lisa sat down with Corduroy on her lap and began to sew
a button on his overalls.
"I like you the way you are," she said, "but you'll be
more comfortable with your shoulder strap fastened."

"You must be a friend," said Corduroy. "I've always wanted a friend."
"Me too!" said Lisa, and gave him a big hug.

# Ferdinand

from *The Story of Ferdinand* by Munro Leaf,
illustrated by Robert Lawson
**THE VIKING PRESS, 1936**

# About Ferdinand

One rainy fall afternoon in 1935, Munro Leaf wrote a story on a yellow legal pad for his out-of-work friend and neighbor, Robert Lawson, to illustrate. He chose a bull because "dogs, rabbits, mice, and goats had all been done a thousand times." In less than an hour, he had composed *The Story of Ferdinand*. It was published in 1936 and retailed for one dollar. Both Leaf and Lawson intended *The Story of Ferdinand* to be a funny tale for children. But adults claimed it for themselves as well and bought Ferdinand hats, underwear, and dolls; women sported hornlike upswept hairdos.

Even more unusual, Ferdinand—who only wanted to "sit just quietly and smell the flowers"—ignited international controversy. Published during the Spanish Civil War, the fable was interpreted as both for and against Generalissimo Francisco Franco. "Everybody saw I was obviously writing propaganda," Leaf said, "but they couldn't decide for which side." Hitler ordered the book burned as "degenerate democratic propaganda." Leaf responded, "If there is a message, it is Ferdinand's message, not mine. It can be understood by babes and graybeards: 'He is very happy.'"

The controversy helped contribute to the book's initial popularity. In 1938, Ferdinand toppled *Gone with the Wind* as the number-one bestseller in the United States.

**Munro Leaf**, 1905–1976, wrote and/or illustrated almost forty children's books. He taught high school and worked as an editor, but his fame will always be for the enduring classic *The Story of Ferdinand*.

**Robert Lawson**, 1892–1957, illustrator of forty-six books, was also the author-illustrator of twenty. *They Were Strong and Good* won the 1941 Caldecott Medal for illustration, and *Rabbit Hill* won the Newbery Medal for literature in 1945. Lawson is the only person to have won both a Caldecott and a Newbery Medal.

Once upon a time in Spain

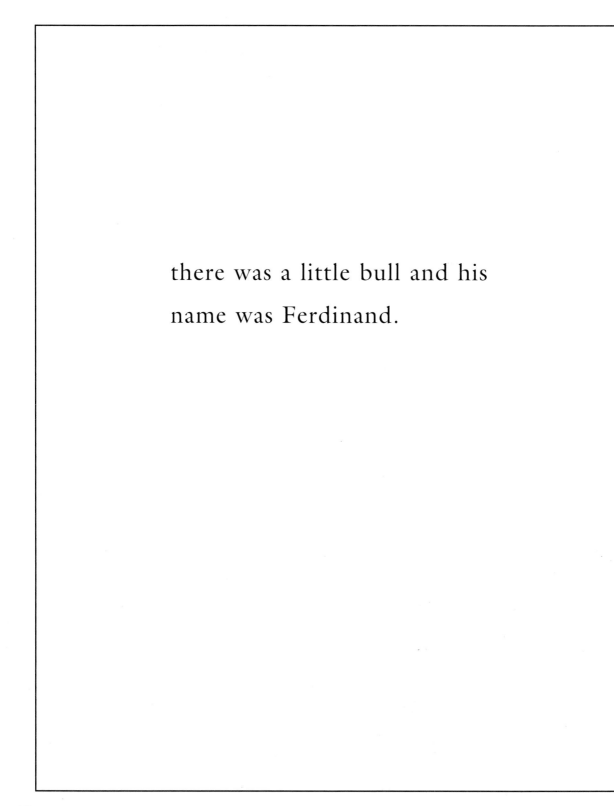

there was a little bull and his
name was Ferdinand.

All the other little bulls he lived with would run and jump and butt their heads together,

but not Ferdinand.

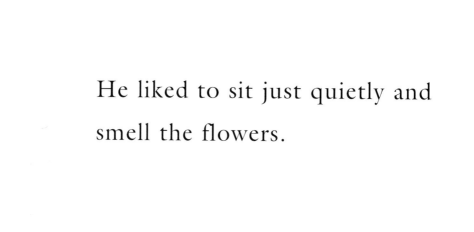

He liked to sit just quietly and smell the flowers.

He had a favorite spot out in the pasture under a cork tree.

It was his favorite tree and he would sit in its shade all day and smell the flowers.

Sometimes his mother, who was a cow, would worry about him. She was afraid he would be lonesome all by himself.

"Why don't you run and play with the other little bulls and skip and butt your head?" she would say.

But Ferdinand would shake his head. "I like it better here where I can sit just quietly and smell the flowers."

His mother saw that he was not lonesome, and because she was an understanding mother, even though she was a cow, she let him just sit there and be happy.

As the years went by Ferdinand grew and grew until he was very big and strong.

All the other bulls who had grown up with him in the same pasture would fight each other all day. They would butt each other and stick each other with their horns. What they wanted most of all was to be picked to fight at the bull fights in Madrid.

But not Ferdinand—he still liked to sit just quietly under the cork tree and smell the flowers.

One day five men came in very funny hats to pick the biggest, fastest, roughest bull to fight in the bull fights in Madrid.

All the other bulls ran around snorting and butting, leaping and jumping so the men would think that they were very very strong and fierce and pick them.

Ferdinand knew that they wouldn't pick him and he didn't care. So he went out to his favorite cork tree to sit down.

RL

He didn't look where he was sitting and instead of sitting on the nice cool grass in the shade he sat on a bumble bee.

Well, if you were a bumble bee and a bull sat on you what would you do? You would sting him. And that is just what this bee did to Ferdinand.

Wow! Did it hurt! Ferdinand jumped up with a snort. He ran around puffing and snorting, butting and pawing the ground as if he were crazy.

RL

The five men saw him and they all shouted with joy. Here was the largest and fiercest bull of all. Just the one for the bull fights in Madrid!

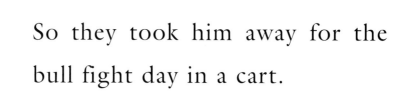

So they took him away for the bull fight day in a cart.

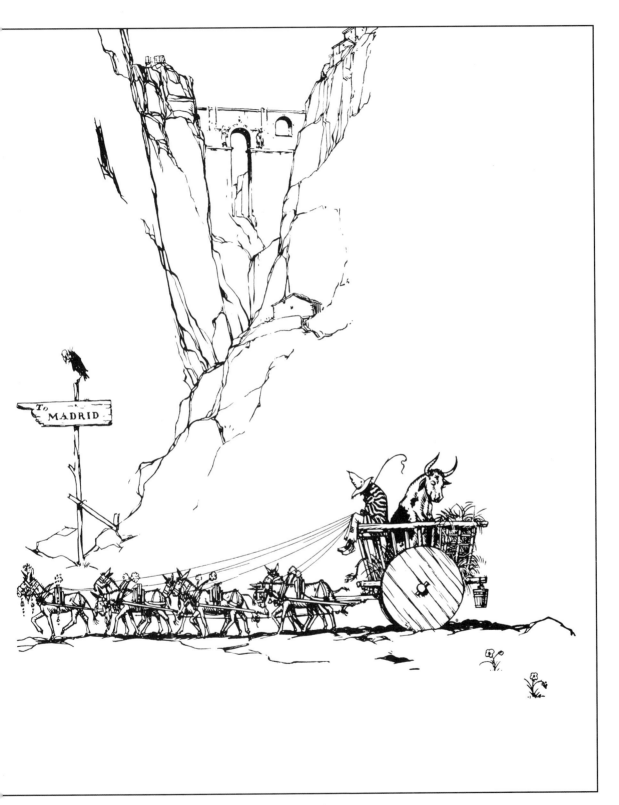

What a day it was! Flags were
flying, bands were playing . . .

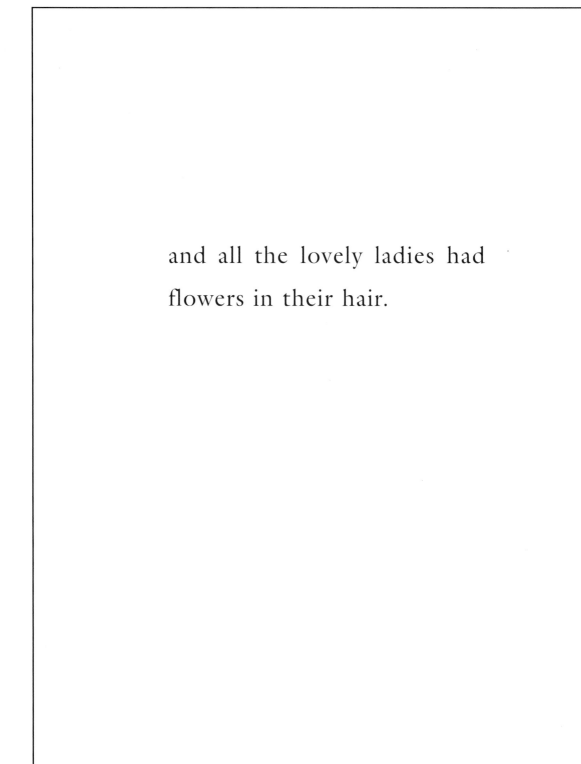

and all the lovely ladies had flowers in their hair.

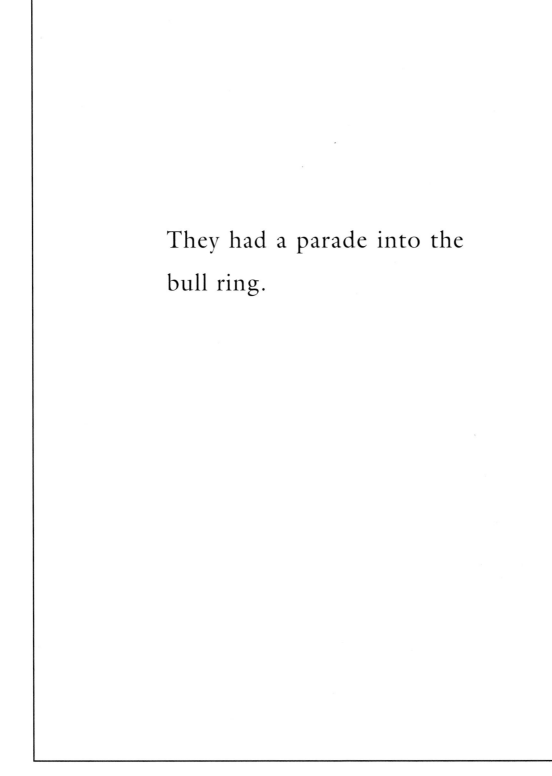

They had a parade into the
bull ring.

Then came the Banderilleros with long sharp pins with ribbons on them to stick in the bull and make him mad.

Next came the Picadores who rode skinny horses and they had long spears to stick in the bull and make him madder.

Then came the Matador, the proudest of all—he thought he was very handsome, and bowed to the ladies. He had a red cape and a sword and was supposed to stick the bull last of all.

Then came the bull, and you
know who that was, don't you?

—FERDINAND.

They called him Ferdinand the Fierce and all the Banderilleros were afraid of him and the Picadores were afraid of him and the Matador was scared stiff.

Ferdinand ran to the middle of the ring and everyone shouted and clapped because they thought he was going to fight fiercely and butt and snort and stick his horns around.

But not Ferdinand. When he got to the middle of the ring he saw the flowers in all the lovely ladies' hair and he just sat down quietly and smelled.

He wouldn't fight and be fierce no matter what they did. He just sat and smelled. And the Banderilleros were mad and the Picadores were madder and the Matador was so mad he cried because he couldn't show off with his cape and sword.

So they had to take Ferdinand home.

And for all I know he is sitting there still, under his favorite cork tree, smelling the flowers just quietly.

He is very happy.

# THE END.

# Pig Pig

from *Pig Pig Gets a Job* by David McPhail
**DUTTON CHILDREN'S BOOKS, 1990**

# About Pig Pig

David McPhail was twenty-six years old when he first read *Charlotte's Web,* by E. B. White, and fell in love with Wilbur. Since then McPhail has always wanted a pig of his own. Although he has lived on farms for a large part of his adult life, he's never owned a pig. "Maybe I've drawn pigs as a way of making up for not having one," McPhail writes.

The creation of Pig Pig, whom *The Horn Book* calls "the most winsome pig in children's literature," occurred in a rather roundabout way. McPhail wrote a story about an old pig who sells all his belongings, buys a small boat with the earnings, and rows off into the sunset. McPhail's editor at the time thought this was "a sad and tragic story—the pig was going off to die." McPhail thought the story was hopeful; Pig Pig was sailing off to the South Seas to begin a new life.

The editor decided not to publish the story, but she was intrigued by the character of Pig Pig and suggested that McPhail write about him as a child. Thus came the first Pig Pig book, *Pig Pig Grows Up.* After its success, more Pig Pig books followed—*Pig Pig Rides, Pig Pig and the Magic Photo Album,* and *Pig Pig Gets a Job*—each one chronicling the adventures and misadventures of that irrepressible, ever-lovable, highly imaginative, and unforgettable pig.

**David McPhail** is the acclaimed author-illustrator of nearly fifty books, and has illustrated more than fifteen others. He has won numerous awards. *Pigs Aplenty, Pigs Galore!* was named an ALA Notable Children's Book. As well as the successful Pig Pig series, McPhail is the creator of *Emma's Vacation, Emma's Pet, The Dream Child, Pigs Ahoy!, Those Can-Do Pigs,* and many other popular children's books. Most recently he collaborated with Jan Waldron on *Angel Pig and the Hidden Christmas.* He lives in Newburyport, Massachusetts.

**O**ne day after school, Pig Pig raced home
to make an announcement.

"I want some money," he told his mother.
"I want to buy something!"

"What do you want to buy, dear?" Pig Pig's
mother asked.

"I don't know yet," Pig Pig answered, "but
something!"

"And what will you do to get this money?"
said his mother.

"Do?" said Pig Pig.

"Do," said his mother. "If you want some money, you must do something to earn it."

"Like work?" squealed Pig Pig. "Like a job?"

"Exactly like," said his mother. "Any ideas?"

Pig Pig thought for a moment.

"Well, I could be a cook!" he said. "I'm good
at making mud pies!"

"You certainly are," his mother agreed, "but not everyone likes mud pies. Maybe you could fix some sandwiches for our lunch."

115

"I could get a job building houses!" said Pig Pig. "I could use the hammer and saw that I got for my birthday!"

"You might start with something small," suggested his mother. "A birdhouse would look nice in the yard."

117

"How about if I get a job as an auto mechanic!"
said Pig Pig. "I could fix race cars when they
break!"

"You could wash them and keep them shiny, too," his mother pointed out. "In fact, *our* car could stand a good cleaning."

119

"Or I could get a job at the dump," said Pig Pig,
"picking up trash and crushing it!"

"Picking up your room would be good practice,"
urged his mother. "But please don't crush anything."

Pig Pig thought of yet another job.
"I could work in the circus," he said, "taking
care of the animals—training them and stuff."

"Stuff like feeding them?" Pig Pig's
mother asked. "And speaking of animals,
has Willie had his supper yet?"

"I have a great idea!" shouted Pig Pig.
"You could give me a job!"

"I could," his mother replied. "But what
can you do?"

"Do?" cried Pig Pig. "Why, I can do plenty! I can feed Willie every day, and clean my room, and wash the car and fix it when it breaks down—"

"Washing it will be enough,"
interrupted his mother. "Is there
anything else?"

"There sure is!" Pig Pig went on.

"I can fix lunch sometimes,
and build things when we need them,

like a bookcase—or a birdhouse!"

"Splendid!" said Pig Pig's mother. "I could pay you, and you would have money to save or to buy something you want."

"And we could call all those things . . . my JOB!"
said Pig Pig proudly.

"We could," said his mother, "and we will!"

And they did.

# Madeline

from *Madeline* by Ludwig Bemelmans
**THE VIKING PRESS, 1939**

# About Madeline

Ludwig Bemelmans spent the summer of 1938 with his wife, Madeleine, and daughter, Barbara, on the Île d'Yeu, off the west coast of France. Part of that summer was spent in the hospital, after Bemelmans's bicycle collided with the one and only car on the small island. Bemelmans wrote, "I was put into a small white carbolicky bed. In the next room was a little girl who had had her appendix out, and on the ceiling over my bed was a crack that, in the varying light of morning, noon, and evening, looked like a rabbit. . . . I saw the nun bringing soup to the little girl. I remembered the stories my mother had told me of life in a convent school and the little girl, the hospital, the room, the crank on the bed, the nurse . . . all fell into place. [Then] I thought about where Madeline and her friends should live and decided on Paris."

**Ludwig Bemelmans** (1898–1962) was a painter, illustrator, and writer of more than three dozen books for both children and adults. A world traveler, Bemelmans was renowned as a true cosmopolite, an irreverent and droll chronicler of the incongruous, an elegant man-about-town, a merry observer of the improbable and the absurd. He died in 1962 after completing the sixth story about Madeline, *Madeline's Christmas.*

In an old house in Paris
that was covered with vines

lived twelve little girls in two straight lines.

In two straight lines they broke their bread

and brushed their teeth

and went to bed.

They smiled at the good

and frowned at the bad

and sometimes they were very sad.

They left the house
at half past nine
in two straight lines

in rain

or shine—

the smallest one was Madeline.

She was not afraid of mice—

she loved winter, snow, and ice.

To the tiger in the zoo
Madeline just said, "Pooh-pooh,"

and nobody knew so well
how to frighten Miss Clavel.

In the middle of one night
Miss Clavel turned on her light
and said, "Something is not right!"

Little Madeline sat in bed,
cried and cried; her eyes were red.

And soon after Dr. Cohn
came, he rushed out to the phone

and he dialed: DANton-ten-six—

"Nurse," he said, "it's an appendix!"

Everybody had to cry—
not a single eye was dry.

Madeline was in his arm
in a blanket safe and warm.

In a car with a red light
they drove out into the night.

Madeline woke up two hours
later, in a room with flowers.

Madeline soon ate and drank.
On her bed there was a crank,

and a crack on the ceiling had the habit
of sometimes looking like a rabbit.

Outside were birds, trees, and sky—
and so ten days passed quickly by.

One nice morning Miss Clavel said—
"Isn't this a fine—

day to visit

Madeline."

## VISITORS FROM TWO TO FOUR
read a sign outside her door.

Tiptoeing with solemn face,
with some flowers and a vase,

in they walked and then said, "Ahhh,"
when they saw the toys and candy
and the dollhouse from Papa.

But the biggest surprise by far—
*on her stomach
was a scar!*

"Good-by," they said, "we'll come again,"

and the little girls left in the rain.

They went home and broke their bread

brushed their teeth

and went to bed.

In the middle of the night
Miss Clavel turned on the light
and said, "Something is not right!"

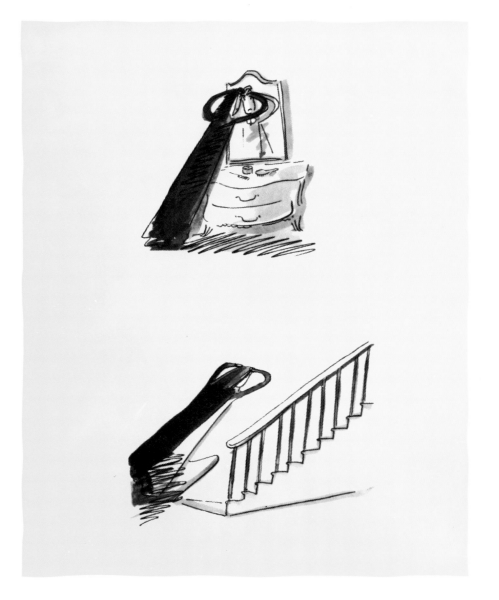

And afraid of a disaster

Miss Clavel ran fast

and faster,

and she said, "Please children do—
tell me what is troubling you?"

And all the little girls cried, "Boohoo,
we want to have our appendix out, too!"

"Good night, little girls!
Thank the lord you are well!
And now go to sleep!"
said Miss Clavel.
And she turned out the light—
and closed the door—
and that's all there is—
there isn't any more.

# Miss Rumphius

from *Miss Rumphius* by Barbara Cooney
**THE VIKING PRESS, 1982**

# About Miss Rumphius

Barbara Cooney has illustrated over one hundred books for children. But "of all the books I have done," she says, "*Miss Rumphius* has been, perhaps, the closest to my heart." Like Miss Rumphius, Barbara Cooney has traveled the world, and eventually settled down by the sea, in Maine, where she tries to make the world more beautiful. And though her popular character is "as near as I ever will come to an autobiography," Miss Rumphius was inspired in part by a real person: a Maine woman who really *did* scatter lupine seeds around her hometown, earning the nickname "Lupine Lady." In 1989, the Maine Library Association established the Lupine Award—taking its name from the glorious landscape depicted in *Miss Rumphius*—which recognizes outstanding children's books by state residents. The first Lupine Award was given to Barbara Cooney for *Miss Rumphius,* and the author was declared a State Treasure by the governor of Maine in 1996.

**Barbara Cooney** was born in 1917 in a hotel built by her grandfather. After growing up on the East Coast, she attended Smith College, where she studied art and art history. Her first book, *Ake and His World,* by Bertil Malmberg, was published in 1940. Ms. Cooney did a short stint as a WAC in Iowa during World War II, but returned to New England, where she and her husband raised four children. Over the course of the next fifty years, she won dozens of awards, including two Caldecott Medals, for *Chanticleer and the Fox* in 1959 and for *Ox-Cart Man,* by Donald Hall, in 1979. More award-winning books followed, including *Island Boy* (1988), *Hattie and the Wild Waves* (1990), *Emily* (Doubleday, 1992), *The Remarkable Christmas of the Cobbler's Son* (1994), and *Eleanor* (1996).

Today, Ms. Cooney lives and works in a house overlooking the sea. "My heart still skips a beat when I look at the sea's horizon. Adventure, magic, all possibilities lie beyond it." There, sitting at her immense drawing table, Barbara Cooney continues to work away. "I plan," she says, "to live to be one hundred years old."

The Lupine Lady lives in a small house overlooking the sea. In between the rocks around her house grow blue and purple and rose-colored flowers. The Lupine Lady is little and old. But she has not always been that way. I know. She is my great-aunt, and she told me so.

Once upon a time she was a little girl named Alice, who lived in a city by the sea. From the front stoop she could see the wharves and the bristling masts of tall ships. Many years ago her grandfather had come to America on a large sailing ship.

Now he worked in the shop at the bottom of the house, making figure-heads for the prows of ships, carving Indians out of wood to put in front of cigar stores. For Alice's grandfather was an artist. He painted pictures, too, of sailing ships and places across the sea. When he was very busy, Alice helped him put in the skies.

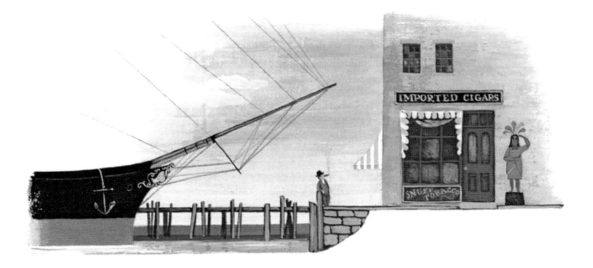

In the evening Alice sat on her grandfather's knee and listened to his stories of faraway places. When he had finished, Alice would say, "When I grow up, I too will go to faraway places, and when I grow old, I too will live beside the sea."

"That is all very well, little Alice," said her grandfather, "but there is a third thing you must do."

"What is that?" asked Alice.

"You must do something to make the world more beautiful," said her grandfather.

"All right," said Alice. But she did not know what that could be.

In the meantime Alice got up and washed her face and ate porridge for breakfast. She went to school and came home and did her homework.

And pretty soon she was grown up.

Then my Great-aunt Alice set out to do the three things she had told her grandfather she was going to do. She left home and went to live in another city far from the sea and salt air. There she worked in a library, dusting books and keeping them from getting mixed up, and helping people find the ones they wanted. Some of the books told her about faraway places.

People called her Miss Rumphius now.

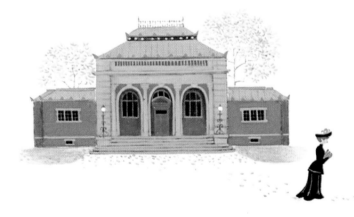

Sometimes she went to the conservatory in the middle of the park. When she stepped inside on a wintry day, the warm moist air wrapped itself around her, and the sweet smell of jasmine filled her nose.

"This is almost like a tropical isle," said Miss Rumphius. "But not quite."

So Miss Rumphius went to a real tropical island, where people kept cockatoos and monkeys as pets. She walked on long beaches, picking up beautiful shells. One day she met the Bapa Raja, king of a fishing village.

"You must be tired," he said. "Come into my house and rest."

So Miss Rumphius went in and met the Bapa Raja's wife. The Bapa Raja himself fetched a green coconut and cut a slice off the top so that Miss Rumphius could drink the coconut water inside. Before she left, the Bapa Raja gave her a beautiful mother-of-pearl shell on which he had painted a bird of paradise and the words, "You will always remain in my heart."

"You will always remain in mine, too," said Miss Rumphius.

My great-aunt Miss Alice Rumphius climbed tall mountains where the snow never melted. She went through jungles and across deserts. She saw lions playing and kangaroos jumping. And everywhere she made friends she would never forget. Finally she came to the Land of the Lotus-Eaters, and there, getting off a camel, she hurt her back.

"What a foolish thing to do," said Miss Rumphius. "Well, I have certainly seen faraway places. Maybe it is time to find my place by the sea."

And it was, and she did.

From the porch of her new house Miss Rumphius watched the sun come up; she watched it cross the heavens and sparkle on the water; and she saw it set in glory in the evening. She started a little garden among the rocks that surrounded her house, and she planted a few flower seeds in the stony ground. Miss Rumphius was almost perfectly happy.

"But there is still one more thing I have to do," she said. "I have to do something to make the world more beautiful."

But what? "The world already is pretty nice," she thought, looking out over the ocean.

The next spring Miss Rumphius was not very well. Her back was bothering her again, and she had to stay in bed most of the time.

The flowers she had planted the summer before had come up and bloomed in spite of the stony ground. She could see them from her bedroom window, blue and purple and rose-colored.

"Lupines," said Miss Rumphius with satisfaction. "I have always loved lupines the best. I wish I could plant more seeds this summer so that I could have still more flowers next year."

But she was not able to.

After a hard winter spring came. Miss Rumphius was feeling much better. Now she could take walks again. One afternoon she started to go up and over the hill, where she had not been in a long time.

"I don't believe my eyes!" she cried when she got to the top. For there on the other side of the hill was a large patch of blue and purple and rose-colored lupines!

"It was the wind," she said as she knelt in delight. "It was the wind that brought the seeds from my garden here! And the birds must have helped!"

Then Miss Rumphius had a wonderful idea!

She hurried home and got out her seed catalogues. She sent off to the very best seed house for five bushels of lupine seed.

All that summer Miss Rumphius, her pockets full of seeds, wandered over fields and headlands, sowing lupines. She scattered seeds along the highways and down the country lanes. She flung handfuls of them around the schoolhouse and back of the church. She tossed them into hollows and along stone walls.

Her back didn't hurt her any more at all.

Now some people called her That Crazy Old Lady.

The next spring there were lupines everywhere. Fields and hillsides were covered with blue and purple and rose-colored flowers. They bloomed along the highways and down the lanes. Bright patches lay around the schoolhouse

and back of the church. Down in the hollows and along the stone walls grew the beautiful flowers.

Miss Rumphius had done the third, most difficult thing of all!

My Great-aunt Alice, Miss Rumphius, is very old now. Her hair is very white. Every year there are more and more lupines. Now they call her the Lupine Lady. Sometimes my friends stand with me outside her gate, curious to see the old, old lady who planted the fields of lupines. When she invites us in, they come slowly. They think she is the oldest woman in the world. Often she tells us stories of faraway places.

"When I grow up," I tell her, "I too will go to faraway places and come home to live by the sea."

"That is all very well, little Alice," says my aunt, "but there is a third thing you must do."

"What is that?" I ask.

"You must do something to make the world more beautiful."

"All right," I say.

But I do not know yet
what that can be.

With thanks
to Hilda

# Peter Rabbit

from *The Tale of Peter Rabbit* by Beatrix Potter
**FREDERICK WARNE & CO., 1902**

# About Peter Rabbit

In September 1893, Beatrix Potter was on holiday in Perthshire, Scotland. Five-year-old Noel Moore, the eldest of her former governess's children, had been ill, and to cheer him, Beatrix sent him a letter. "My dear Noel, I don't know what to write to you, so I shall tell you a story. . . ." The letter was eight pages long, and full of little pictures. Told for the first time, it was a story that was to become popular all over the world—*The Tale of Peter Rabbit*.

During the next few years, Beatrix began to earn a little money by selling designs for greeting cards and illustrated books. Her success at this convinced her to try to get her story of four little rabbits published. At least six publishers rejected Beatrix's manuscript before she decided to publish it herself in a run of 250 copies in December 1901. The private printing was such a success that Frederick Warne & Co. agreed to reconsider the manuscript and decided to publish *The Tale of Peter Rabbit* if Beatrix would reillustrate the whole book in color. The first commercial edition was published in October 1902 and by the end of December, there were more than 28,000 copies in print. *The Tale of Peter Rabbit* is now a worldwide bestseller, translated into thirty languages, and a favorite of children and parents everywhere.

**Beatrix Potter**, 1866–1943, was the author and illustrator of the twenty-three storybooks known as The Original Peter Rabbit Books as well as other stories for children. She was raised in London but very early developed a keen interest in the countryside and the natural sciences. Her extremely accomplished scientific observation and illustration formed the basis for the detailed and accurate animal characters that populate her books for children. After the success of *The Tale of Peter Rabbit*, Beatrix was able in 1905 to purchase Hill Top, a farm in England's Lake District. Over the years, the Lake District became her permanent home, and she acquired several more properties, where she farmed and raised sheep. When she died in 1943, Beatrix left her land and farms to the National Trust.

ONCE upon a time there were four little Rabbits, and their names were—
                    Flopsy,
            Mopsy,
        Cotton-tail,
    and Peter.
They lived with their Mother in a sand-bank, underneath the root of
        a very big fir-tree.
            "Now, my dears,"
        said old Mrs. Rabbit one morning,
            "you may go into the fields or
                down the lane, but don't go into
                    Mr. McGregor's garden: your
                    Father had an accident there;
                    he was put in a pie by Mrs.
                    McGregor.

"Now run along, and don't get into mischief. I am going out."

Then old Mrs. Rabbit took a basket and her umbrella, and went through the wood to the baker's. She bought a loaf of brown bread and five currant buns.

Flopsy, Mopsy, and Cotton-tail, who were good little bunnies, went down the lane to gather blackberries.

But Peter, who was very naughty, ran straight away to Mr. McGregor's garden, and squeezed under the gate!

First he ate some lettuces and some French beans; and then he ate some radishes.

And then, feeling rather sick, he went to look for some parsley.

But round the end of a cucumber frame, whom should he meet but Mr. McGregor!

Mr. McGregor was on his hands and knees planting out young cabbages, but he jumped up and ran after Peter, waving a rake and calling out, "Stop thief!"

Peter was most dreadfully frightened; he rushed all over the garden, for he had forgotten the way back to the gate.

He lost one of his shoes among the cabbages, and the other shoe amongst the potatoes.

After losing them, he ran on four legs and went faster, so that I think he might have got away altogether if he had not unfortunately run into a gooseberry net, and got caught by the large buttons on his jacket.

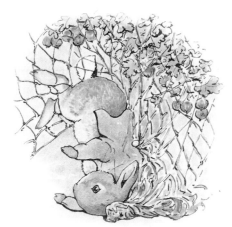

It was a blue jacket with brass buttons, quite new.

Peter gave himself up for lost, and shed big tears; but his sobs were overheard by some friendly sparrows, who flew to him in great excitement, and implored him to exert himself.

Mr. McGregor came up with a sieve, which he intended to pop upon the top of Peter; but Peter wriggled out just in time, leaving his jacket behind him.

And rushed into the tool-shed, and jumped into a can. It would have been a beautiful thing to hide in, if it had not had so much water in it.

Mr. McGregor was quite sure that Peter was somewhere in the tool-shed, perhaps hidden underneath a flower-pot. He began to turn them over carefully, looking under each.

Presently Peter sneezed— "Kertyschoo!" Mr. McGregor was after him in no time.

And tried to put his foot upon Peter,
who jumped out of a window, upsetting
three plants. The window was too
small for Mr. McGregor, and he
was tired of running after Peter.
He went back to his work.

Peter sat down to rest; he was
out of breath and trembling with
fright, and he had not the least
idea which way to go.

Also he was very damp with sitting
in that can.

After a time he began to wander
about, going lippity—lippity—not
very fast, and
looking all
round.

He found a door in a wall; but it was
locked, and there was no room for a fat
little rabbit to squeeze underneath.

An old mouse was running in and out
over the stone door-step, carrying peas and
beans to her family in the wood. Peter asked
her the way to the gate, but she had such a large
pea in her mouth that she could not answer. She only shook
her head at him. Peter began to cry.

Then he tried to find his way straight across the garden, but he became more and more puzzled. Presently, he came to a pond where Mr. McGregor filled his water-cans. A white cat was staring at some gold-fish, she sat very, very still, but now and then the tip of her tail twitched as if it were alive. Peter thought it best to go away without speaking to her; he had heard about cats from his cousin, little Benjamin Bunny.

He went back towards the tool-shed, but suddenly, quite close to him, he heard the noise of a hoe —scr-r-ritch, scratch, scratch, scritch. Peter scuttered underneath the bushes. But presently, as nothing happened, he came out, and climbed upon a wheelbarrow and peeped over. The first thing he saw was Mr. McGregor hoeing onions. His back was turned towards Peter, and beyond him was the gate!

Peter got down very quietly off the wheelbarrow, and started running as fast as he could go, along a straight walk behind some black-currant bushes.

Mr. McGregor caught sight of him at the corner, but Peter did not care. He slipped underneath the gate, and was safe at last in the wood outside the garden.

Mr. McGregor hung up the little jacket and the shoes for a scarecrow to frighten the blackbirds.

Peter never stopped running or looked behind him till he got home to the big fir-tree.

He was so tired that he flopped down upon the nice soft sand on the floor of the rabbit-hole and shut his eyes. His mother was busy cooking; she wondered what he had done with his clothes. It was the second little jacket and pair of shoes that Peter had lost in a fortnight!

I am sorry to say that Peter was not very well during the evening.

His mother put him to bed, and made some camomile tea; and she gave a dose of it to Peter!

"One table-spoonful to be taken at bed-time."

But Flopsy, Mopsy, and Cotton-tail had bread and milk and black-berries for supper.

THE END

# Winnie-the-Pooh

from *Winnie-the-Pooh* and *Now We Are Six* by A. A. Milne,
illustrated by Ernest H. Shepard

**E. P. DUTTON & CO., INC. 1926, 1927**

# About Winnie-the-Pooh

More than seventy years have passed since Winnie-the-Pooh first came down the stairs *bump, bump, bump* on the back of his head behind Christopher Robin. Since then, the Beloved Bear of Little Brain has charmed children and adults alike with his heartwarming simplicity and naive charm. In addition to the four original books, Pooh has appeared in dozens of other works, and on video, radio, television, and on the stage. His image has graced items ranging from pottery to postage stamps. That *Winnie-the-Pooh* has been translated into thirty-one languages is testament to the literary legend that is Pooh, truly the Best Bear in All the World.

**A. A. Milne** (1882–1956) was born in England, the third and youngest son of London schoolteachers. He began writing as a schoolboy and went on to edit the school newspaper in college. He then worked as an editor at *Punch* magazine for eight years. In 1913 he married Dorothy (Daphne) de Selincourt. Their son, Christopher Robin, was born in 1920. It was Daphne who first suggested that the child's toys—a stuffed bear, tiger, pig, and donkey—become characters in a children's book. *Winnie-the-Pooh* was published in 1926, promptly establishing Milne as a major author of children's books. It was followed in 1928 by *The House At Pooh Corner*, which was also a great success. Milne also wrote two collections of verse for children, *When We Were Very Young* (1924) and *Now We Are Six* (1927).

**Ernest H. Shepard** (1879–1976) was born in London. As a boy, he loved to paint and draw and planned to be an artist. His first picture was exhibited at the Royal Academy in 1901. In 1903 he married Florence Chaplin. They had two children—Mary, who later illustrated the Mary Poppins books, and Graham, who was killed in World War II. Shepard served in Europe during the war. Afterward he joined the editorial board at *Punch*, where he met A. A. Milne. In addition to the four original Pooh books, Shepard illustrated many other books for adults and children, among them Kenneth Grahame's *The Wind in the Willows*.

# Winnie-the-Pooh and Some Bees

Here is Edward Bear, coming downstairs now, bump, bump, bump, on the back of his head, behind Christopher Robin. It is, as far as he knows, the only way of coming downstairs, but sometimes he feels that there really is another way, if only he could stop bumping for a moment and think of it. And then he feels that perhaps there isn't. Anyhow, here he is at the bottom, and ready to be introduced to you. Winnie-the-Pooh.

When I first heard his name, I said, just as you are going to say, "But I thought he was a boy?"

"So did I," said Christopher Robin.

"Then you can't call him Winnie?"

"I don't."

"But you said——"

"He's Winnie-ther-Pooh. Don't you know what *'ther'* means?"

"Ah, yes, now I do," I said quickly; and I hope you do too, because it is all the explanation you are going to get.

Sometimes Winnie-the-Pooh likes a game of some sort when he comes downstairs, and sometimes he likes to sit quietly in front of the fire and listen to a story. This evening——

"What about a story?" said Christopher Robin.

"*What* about a story?" I said.

"Could you very sweetly tell Winnie-the-Pooh one?"

"I suppose I could," I said. "What sort of stories does he like?"

"About himself. Because he's *that* sort of Bear."

"Oh, I see."

"So could you very sweetly?"

"I'll try," I said.

So I tried.

Once upon a time, a very long time ago now, about last Friday, Winnie-the-Pooh lived in a forest all by himself under the name of Sanders.

(*"What does 'under the name' mean?" asked Christopher Robin.*

*"It means he had the name over the door in gold letters, and lived under it."*

*"Winnie-the-Pooh wasn't quite sure," said Christopher Robin.*

*"Now I am," said a growly voice.*

*"Then I will go on," said I.*)

One day when he was out walking, he came to an open place in the middle of the forest, and in the middle of this place was a large oak-tree, and, from the top of the tree, there came a loud buzzing-noise.

Winnie-the-Pooh sat down at the foot of the tree, put his head between his paws and began to think.

First of all he said to himself: "That buzzing-noise means something. You don't get a buzzing-noise like that, just buzzing and buzzing, without

its meaning something. If there's a buzzing-noise, somebody's making a buzzing-noise, and the only reason for making a buzzing-noise that *I* know of is because you're a bee."

Then he thought another long time, and said: "And the only reason for being a bee that I know of is making honey."

And then he got up, and said: "And the only reason for making honey is so as *I* can eat it." So he began to climb the tree.

He
climbed
and
he
climbed
and
he
climbed,
and
as
he
climbed
he
sang
a
little
song
to
himself.
It
went
like
this:

Isn't it funny
How a bear likes honey?
Buzz! Buzz! Buzz!
I wonder why he does?

Then he climbed a little further . . . and a little further . . . and then just a little further. By that time he had thought of another song.

> It's a very funny thought that, if Bears were Bees,
> They'd build their nests at the *bottom* of trees.
> And that being so (if the Bees were Bears),
> We shouldn't have to climb up all these stairs.

He was getting rather tired by this time, so that is why he sang a Complaining Song. He was nearly there now, and if he just stood on that branch . . .
*Crack!*

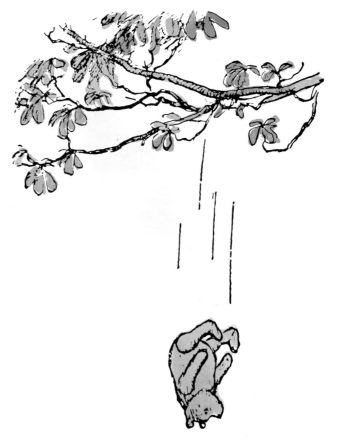

"Oh, help!" said Pooh, as he dropped ten feet on the branch below him.

"If only I hadn't——" he said, as he bounced twenty feet on to the next branch.

"You see, what I *meant* to do," he explained, as he turned head-over-heels, and crashed on to another branch thirty feet below, "what I *meant* to do——"

"Of course, it *was* rather——" he admitted, as he slithered very quickly through the next six branches.

"It all comes, I suppose," he decided, as he said good-bye to the last branch, spun round three times, and flew gracefully into a gorse-bush, "it all comes of *liking* honey so much. Oh, help!"

He crawled out of the gorse-bush, brushed the prickles from his nose, and began to think again. And the first person he thought of was Christopher Robin.

*("Was that me?" said Christopher Robin in an awed voice, hardly daring to believe it.*
*"That was you."*
*Christopher Robin said nothing, but his eyes got larger and larger, and his face got pinker and pinker.)*

So Winnie-the-Pooh went round to his friend
Christopher Robin, who lived behind a green
door in another part of the forest.

"Good morning, Christopher Robin," he said.

"Good morning, Winnie-*ther*-Pooh," said you.

"I wonder if you've got such a thing as a balloon about you?"

"A balloon?"

"Yes, I just said to myself coming along: 'I wonder if Christopher Robin has such a thing as a balloon about him?' I just said it to myself, thinking of balloons, and wondering."

"What do you want a balloon for?" you said.

Winnie-the-Pooh looked round to see that nobody was listening, put his paw to his mouth, and said in a deep whisper: *"Honey!"*

"But you don't get honey with balloons!"

"*I* do," said Pooh.

Well, it just happened that you had been to a party the day before at the house of your friend Piglet, and you had balloons at the party. You had had a big green balloon; and one of Rabbit's relations had had a big blue one, and had left it behind, being really too young to go to a party at all; and so you had brought the green one *and* the blue one home with you.

"Which one would you like?" you asked Pooh.

He put his head between his paws and thought very carefully.

"It's like this," he said. "When you go after honey with a balloon, the great thing is not to let the bees know you're coming. Now, if you have a green balloon, they might think you were only part of the tree, and not notice you, and if you have a blue balloon, they might think you were only part of the sky, and not notice you, and the question is: Which is most likely?"

"Wouldn't they notice *you* underneath the balloon?" you asked.

"They might or they might not," said Winnie-the-Pooh. "You never can tell with bees." He thought for a moment and said: "I shall try to look like a small black cloud. That will deceive them."

"Then you had better have the blue balloon," you said; and so it was decided.

Well, you both went out with the blue balloon, and you took your gun with you, just in case, as you always did, and Winnie-the-Pooh went to a very muddy place that he knew of, and rolled and rolled until he was black all over; and then, when the balloon was blown up as big as big, and you

and Pooh were both holding on to the string, you let go suddenly, and Pooh Bear floated gracefully up into the sky, and stayed there—level with the top of the tree and about twenty feet away from it.

"Hooray!" you shouted.

"Isn't that fine?" shouted Winnie-the-Pooh down to you. "What do I look like?"

"You look like a Bear holding on to a balloon," you said.

"Not—" said Pooh anxiously, "—not like a small black cloud in a blue sky?"

"Not very much."

"Ah, well, perhaps from up here it looks different. And, as I say, you never can tell with bees."

There was no wind to blow him nearer to the tree, so there he stayed. He could see the honey, he could smell the honey, but he couldn't quite reach the honey.

After a little while he called down to you.

"Christopher Robin!" he said in a loud whisper.

"Hallo!"

"I think the bees *suspect* something!"

"What sort of thing?"

"I don't know. But something tells me that they're *suspicious*!"

"Perhaps they think that you're after their honey."

"It may be that. You never can tell with bees."

There was another little silence, and then he called down to you again.

"Christopher Robin!"

"Yes?"

"Have you an umbrella in your house?"

"I think so."

"I wish you would bring it out here, and walk up and down with it, and look up at me every now and then, and say 'Tut-tut, it looks like rain.' I think, if you did that, it would help the deception which we are practising on these bees."

Well, you laughed to yourself, "Silly old Bear!" but you didn't say it aloud because you were so fond of him, and you went home for your umbrella.

"Oh, there you are!" called down Winnie-the-Pooh, as soon as you got back to the tree. "I was beginning to get anxious. I have discovered that the bees are now definitely Suspicious."

"Shall I put my umbrella up?" you said.

"Yes, but wait a moment. We must be practical. The important bee to deceive is the Queen Bee. Can you see which is the Queen Bee from down there?"

"No."

"A pity. Well, now, if you walk up and down with your umbrella, saying, 'Tut-tut, it looks like rain,' I shall do what I can by singing a little Cloud Song, such as a cloud might sing. . . . Go!"

So, while you walked up and down and wondered if it would rain, Winnie-the-Pooh sang this
song:

> How sweet to be a Cloud
>     Floating in the Blue!
> Every little cloud
> *Always* sings aloud.

> "How sweet to be a Cloud
>     Floating in the Blue!"
> It makes him very proud
> To be a little cloud.

The bees were still buzzing as suspiciously as
ever. Some of them, indeed, left their nest and flew

all round the cloud as it began the second verse of this song, and one bee sat down on the nose of the cloud for a moment, and then got up again.

"Christopher—*ow!*—Robin," called out the cloud.

"Yes?"

"I have just been thinking, and I have come to a very important decision. *These are the wrong sort of bees.*"

"Are they?"

"Quite the wrong sort. So I should think they would make the wrong sort of honey, shouldn't you?"

"Would they?"

"Yes. So I think I shall come down."

"How?" asked you.

Winnie-the-Pooh hadn't thought about this. If he let go of the string, he would fall—*bump*—and he didn't like the idea of that. So he thought for a long time, and then he said:

"Christopher Robin, you must shoot the balloon with your gun. Have you got your gun?"

"Of course I have," you said. "But if I do that, it will spoil the balloon," you said.

"But if you *don't*," said Pooh, "I shall have to let go, and that would spoil *me*."

When you put it like this, you saw how it was, and you aimed very carefully at the balloon, and fired.

"*Ow!*" said Pooh.

"Did I miss?" you asked.

"You didn't exactly *miss,*" said Pooh, "but you missed the *balloon.*"

"I'm so sorry," you said, and you fired again, and this time you hit the balloon, and the air came slowly out, and Winnie-the-Pooh floated down to the ground.

But his arms were so stiff from holding on to the string of the balloon all that time that they stayed up straight in the air for more than a week, and whenever a fly came and settled on his nose he had to blow it off. And I think—but I am not sure—that *that* is why he was always called Pooh.

"Is that the end of the story?" asked Christopher Robin.

"That's the end of that one. There are others."

"About Pooh and Me?"

"And Piglet and Rabbit and all of you. Don't you remember?"

"I do remember, and then when I try to remember, I forget."

"That day when Pooh and Piglet tried to catch the Heffalump——"

"They didn't catch it, did they?"

"No."

"Pooh couldn't, because he hasn't any brain. Did *I* catch it?"

"Well, that comes into the story."

Christopher Robin nodded.

"I do remember," he said, "only Pooh doesn't very well, so that's why he likes having it told to him again. Because then it's a real story and not just a remembering."

"That's just how *I* feel," I said.

Christopher Robin gave a deep sigh, picked his Bear up by the leg, and walked off to the door, trailing Pooh behind him. At the door he turned and said, "Coming to see me have my bath?"

"I might," I said.

"I didn't hurt him when I shot him, did I?"

"Not a bit."

He nodded and went out, and in a moment I heard Winnie-the-Pooh—*bump, bump, bump*—going up the stairs behind him.

## Us Two

Wherever I am, there's always Pooh,
There's always Pooh and Me.
Whatever I do, he wants to do,
"Where are you going today?" says Pooh:
"Well, that's very odd 'cos I was too.
Let's go together," says Pooh, says he.
"Let's go together," says Pooh.

"What's twice eleven?" I said to Pooh.
("Twice what?" said Pooh to Me.)
"I *think* it ought to be twenty-two."
"Just what I think myself," said Pooh.
"It wasn't an easy sum to do,
But that's what it is," said Pooh, said he.
"That's what it is," said Pooh.

"Let's look for dragons," I said to Pooh.
"Yes, let's," said Pooh to Me.
We crossed the river and found a few—
"Yes, those are dragons all right," said Pooh.
"As soon as I saw their beaks I knew.
That's what they are," said Pooh, said he.
"That's what they are," said Pooh.

"Let's frighten the dragons," I said to Pooh.
"That's right," said Pooh to Me.
"*I'm* not afraid," I said to Pooh,
And I held his paw and I shouted "Shoo!
Silly old dragons!"—and off they flew.

"I wasn't afraid," said Pooh, said he,
"I'm *never* afraid with you."

So wherever I am, there's always Pooh,
There's always Pooh and Me.
"What would I do?" I said to Pooh,
"If it wasn't for you," and Pooh said: "True,
It isn't much fun for One, but Two
Can stick together," says Pooh, says he.
"That's how it is," says Pooh.

# Fudge

from *Tales of a Fourth Grade Nothing* by Judy Blume,
illustrated by Roy Doty
**DUTTON CHILDREN'S BOOKS, 1972**

# About Fudge

Farley Drexel Hatcher, known to just about everyone as Fudge, makes his first appearance in *Tales of a Fourth Grade Nothing* as the two-and-a-half-year-old terror of his older brother Peter's life. Fudge is the original terrible two—he knocks out his front teeth trying to fly, pretends he's a dog, refuses to eat, and scribbles all over his brother's homework. Nine-year-old Peter can't understand why his parents don't realize that Fudge is ruining his life.

The character of Fudge is based on Judy Blume's own son Larry in his toddler years. Larry was, according to Blume, "an interesting child," who would perform such Fudge-like antics as dumping a bowl of peas on his head in a restaurant. He never swallowed a turtle, though. The idea for that episode came from a newspaper article that Blume read about a child who actually swallowed one.

After the publication of *Tales of a Fourth Grade Nothing,* thousands of readers wrote to Blume asking her to write another book about Fudge and Peter. Two more Fudge books followed—*Superfudge,* in which Fudge is no longer the baby in the Hatcher family, and *Fudge-a-mania,* in which the Hatchers vacation in Maine with Peter's arch-enemy, the Cootie Queen Sheila Tubman (from *Otherwise Known as Sheila the Great*), and her family. Since *Tales of a Fourth Grade Nothing* was published in 1971, Fudge has appeared on television, in movies, and on the stage.

**Judy Blume** is the author of twenty-one books—nineteen for children and young adults and two for adults. She began her career by writing the stories she told her two young children. She wanted to create the kind of books that she wished she could have read as a young girl—honest representations of the joys and traumas of growing up. The warmth and humor of her many books have won her a legion of devoted fans, making her one of the best-loved living authors of children's books. Judy Blume lives in New York City.

# Fudge

Some people might think that my mother is my biggest problem. She doesn't like turtles and she's always telling me to scrub my hands. That doesn't mean just run them under the water. *Scrub* means I'm supposed to use soap and rub my hands together. Then I've got to rinse and dry them. I ought to know by now. I've heard it enough!

But my mother isn't my biggest problem. Neither is my father. He spends a lot of time watching commercials on TV. That's because he's in the advertising business. These days his favorite commercial is the one about Juicy-O. He wrote it himself. And the president of the Juicy-O company liked it so much he sent my father a whole crate of Juicy-O for our family to drink. It tastes like a combination of oranges, pineapples, grapefruits, pears, and bananas. (And if you want to know the truth, I'm getting pretty sick of drinking it.) But Juicy-O isn't my biggest problem either.

My biggest problem is my brother, Farley Drexel Hatcher. He's two-and-a-half years old. Everybody calls him Fudge. I feel sorry for him if he's going to grow up with a name like Fudge, but I don't say a word. It's none of my business.

Fudge is always in my way. He messes up everything he sees. And when he gets mad he throws himself flat on the floor and he screams. *And* he kicks. *And* he bangs his fists.

The only time I really like him is when he's sleeping. He sucks four fingers on his left hand and makes a slurping noise.

When Fudge saw Dribble he said, "Ohhhhh . . . see!"

And I said, "That's *my* turtle, get it? *Mine!* You don't touch him."

Fudge said, "No touch." Then he laughed like crazy.

# The Birthday Bash

I got used to the way Fudge looked without his top front teeth. He looked like a very small first grader. Dr. Brown, our dentist, said he'd have to wait until he was six or seven to get his grown-up teeth. I started calling him Fang because when he smiles all you can see are the top two side teeth next to the big space. So it looks like he has fangs.

My mother didn't like that. "I want you to stop calling him Fang," she told me.

"What should I call him?" I asked. "Farley Drexel?"

"Just plain Fudge will be fine," my mother said.

"What's wrong with Farley Drexel?" I asked. "How come you named him that if you don't like it?"

"I like it fine," my mother said. "But right now we call him Fudge. Not Farley . . . not Drexel . . . and *not* Fang!"

"What's wrong with Fang?" I asked. "I think it sounds neat."

"Fang is an insult!"

"Oh . . . come on, Mom! He doesn't even know what a fang is!"

"But *I* know, Peter. And *I* don't like it."

"Okay . . . okay. . . ." I promised never to call my brother Fang again.

But secretly, whenever I look at him, I think it.

*My brother, Fang Hatcher!* Nobody can stop me from thinking. My mind is my own.

Fudge is going to be three years old. My mother said he should have a birthday party with some of his friends. He plays with three other little kids who live in our building. There's Jennie, Ralph, and Sam. My mother invited them to Fudge's party. Grandma said she'd come over to help. My father couldn't make it. He had a Saturday business appointment. I wanted to go to Jimmy Fargo's but my mother said she needed me to supervise the games. The kids were invited from one until two-thirty.

"That's only an hour and a half," my mother reminded me. "That's not so bad, is it, Peter?"

"I don't know yet," I told her. "Ask me later."

The kitchen table was set up for the party. The cloth and napkins and paper plates and cups all matched. They had pictures of Superman on them.

Right before party time Grandma tried to change Fudge into his new suit. But he screamed his head off about it. "No suit! No suit! NO . . . NO . . . NO!"

My mother tried to reason with him. "It's your birthday, Fudgie. All your friends are coming. You want to look like a big boy, don't you?" While she was talking to him she managed to get him into his shirt and pants. But he wouldn't let her put on his shoes. He kicked and carried on until my mother and grandmother were both black and blue. Finally they decided as long as he was in his suit his feet didn't matter. So he wore his old bedroom slippers.

Ralph arrived first. He's really fat. And he isn't even four years old. He doesn't say much either. He grunts and grabs a lot, though. Usually his mouth is stuffed full of something.

So the first thing Ralph did was wander into the kitchen. He looked around for something to eat. But Grandma was guarding the place. She kept telling him "No

. . . No . . . must wait until the other children come."

Jennie arrived next. She was wearing little white gloves and party shoes. She even carried a pocketbook. Besides that she had on dirty jeans and an old sweater. Her mother apologized for her clothes but said she couldn't do anything with Jennie lately—especially since she had taken to biting.

"What does she bite?" I asked, thinking about furniture or toys or stuff like that.

"She bites people," Jennie's mother said. "But you don't have to worry about it unless her teeth go through the skin. Otherwise it's perfectly safe."

I thought, *poor old Fudge! He can't even bite back since he hasn't got any top front teeth.* I looked at Jennie. She seemed so innocent. It was hard to believe she was a vampire.

Sam came last. He carried a big present for Fudge but he was crying. "It's just a stage he's going through," his mother explained. "Everything scares him. Especially birthday parties. But he'll be fine. Won't you, Sam?"

Sam grabbed onto his mother's leg and screamed, "Take me home! Take me home!" Somehow, Sam's mother untangled herself from Sam's grip and left.

So at five after one we were ready to begin. We had an eater, a biter, and a crier. I thought that two-thirty would never come. I also thought my mother was slightly crazy for dreaming up the party in the first place. "Doesn't Fudge have any normal friends?" I whispered.

"There's nothing wrong with Fudgie's friends!" my mother whispered back. "All small children are like that."

Grandma got them seated around the kitchen table. She put a party hat on each kid's head. Sam screamed, "Get it off! Get it off!" But the others wore their hats and didn't complain. My mother snapped a picture of them with her new camera.

Then Grandma turned off the lights and my mother lit

the candles on Fudge's cake. It had chocolate frosting and big yellow roses. I led the singing of "Happy Birthday." My mother carried the cake across the kitchen to the party table and set it down in front of Fudge.

Sam cried, "Too dark! Too dark!" So Grandma had to turn on the kitchen lights before Fudge blew out his candles. When he was finished blowing he reached out and grabbed a rose off his cake. He shoved it into his mouth.

"Oh, Fudge!" my mother said. "Look what you did."

But Grandma said, "It's his birthday. He can do whatever he wants!"

So Fudge reached over and grabbed a second rose.

I guess fat Ralph couldn't stand seeing Fudge eat those yellow roses because he grabbed one, too. By that time the cake looked pretty messy. My mother, finally coming to her senses, took the cake away and sliced it up.

Each kid got a Dixie Cup, a small piece of cake, and some milk. But Jennie hollered, "Where's my rose? Want one too!" Because her slice of birthday cake didn't happen to have one.

My mother explained that the roses were only decorations and there weren't enough to go around. Jennie seemed to accept that. But when Grandma stood over her to help open her Dixie, Jennie bit her on the hand.

"She bit me!" Grandma cried.

"Did it break the skin?" my mother asked.

"No . . . I don't think so," Grandma said, checking.

"Good. Then it's nothing to worry about," my mother told her.

Grandma went into the bathroom to put some medicine on it anyway. She wasn't taking any chances.

Ralph was the first one to finish his food. "More . . . more . . . more!" he sang, holding up his empty plate.

"I don't think you should give him any more," I whispered to my mother. "Look how fat he is now!"

"Oh, Peter . . . this is a party. Let him eat whatever he wants."

"Okay," I said. "Why should I care how fat he gets?"

My mother served Ralph a second piece of cake. He threw up right after he finished it.

Me and Grandma took the kids into the living room while my mother cleaned up the mess.

Grandma told Fudge he could open his presents while his friends watched. Jennie brought him a musical jack-in-the-box. When you turn the handle around it plays "Pop Goes the Weasel." When you reach the part of the song about Pop, the top opens and a funny clown jumps up. Fudge loved it. He clapped his hands and laughed and laughed. But Sam started to scream, "No! No more. Take it away!" He hid his face in his hands and wouldn't look up until Grandma promised to put the jack-in-the-box in another room.

Fudge opened Ralph's present next. It was a little windup car that ran all over the floor. I kind of liked it myself. So did Ralph. Because he grabbed it away from Fudge and said, "MINE."

"No!" Fudge shouted. "MINE."

When my mother heard the racket she ran in from the kitchen. She explained to Ralph that he had brought the car to Fudge because it was *his* birthday. But Ralph wouldn't listen. I guess my mother was afraid he might throw up again, and this time on the living room rug. So she begged Fudge to let Ralph play with the car for a few minutes. But Ralph kept screaming it was *his* car. So Fudge started to cry. Finally, my mother took the car away and said, "Let's see what Sam brought you."

Fudge liked that idea. He forgot about the little car and ripped the paper and ribbon off Sam's package. It turned out to be a big picture dictionary. The same kind the Yarbys brought me a couple of months ago. Fudge got mad when he saw it.

"No!" he yelled. "NO MORE BOOK!" He threw it across the room.

"Fudge! That's terrible," my mother said. "You mustn't do that to the nice book."

"No book!" Fudge said.

Sam cried, "He doesn't like it. He doesn't like my present. I want to go home . . . I want to go home!"

Grandma tried to comfort Sam while my mother picked up the book. She gathered the wrapping paper and ribbons and cards together. Fudge didn't even look at any of the birthday cards. Oh well, he can't read, so I guess it doesn't make any difference.

"Peter," my mother said, "let's start the games . . . now . . . quick!"

I checked the time. I hoped the party was almost over. But no, it was only one-thirty. Still an hour to go. I went into my room where I had blown up a lot of balloons. My mother has this party book and it says three-year-olds like to dance around with balloons. When I got back to the living room Mom started the record player and I handed each kid a balloon.

But they just stood there looking at me. I thought, *either the guy who wrote that party book is crazy or I am!*

"Show them how, Peter," my mother said. "Take a balloon and demonstrate."

I felt like one of the world's great living fools dancing around with a balloon, but it worked. As soon as the kids saw me doing it, they started dancing too. And the more they danced the more they liked it. Until Jennie's balloon popped. That nearly scared Sam right out of his mind. He started yelling and crying. Fortunately I had blown up two dozen balloons. I was hoping they'd dance around the rest of the afternoon.

Fudge got the idea of jumping up and down on the furniture. The others liked that too. So instead of dancing with their balloons, that's what they did. And soon they were running from room to room, yelling and laughing and having a great time.

Then the doorbell rang. It was Mrs. Rudder. She lives in the apartment right under us. She wanted to know what was going on. She said it sounded like her ceiling was about to crash in on her any second.

My mother explained that Fudge was having a little birthday party and wouldn't she like to stay for a piece of cake? Sometimes my mother is really clever! So Grandma entertained Mrs. Rudder in the kitchen while Fudge and his buddies jumped up and down on his new bed.

It was delivered this morning. Fudge hasn't even slept in it yet. So naturally when my mother found out what they were up to, she was mad. "Stop it right now!" she said.

"New bed . . . big boy!" Fudge told her. Was he proud!

"You won't have a new-big-boy-bed for long if you don't stop jumping on it," my mother told him. "I know . . . let's all sit down on the floor and hear a nice story." My mother selected a picture book from Fudge's bookshelf.

"I heard that one!" Jennie said when she saw the cover.

"All right," my mother told her, "let's hear this one." She held up another book.

"I heard that one too," Jennie said.

I think my mother was starting to lose her patience. But she chose a third book and said, "We'll all enjoy this one even if we know it by heart. And if we *do* know it by heart . . . well, we can say it together."

That's just what Jennie did. And when my mother skipped a page by mistake Jennie was right there to remind her. If you ask me, my mother felt like biting Jennie by that time!

When the story was over it was two o'clock and Ralph

was sound asleep on the floor. My mother told me to put him up on Fudge's new bed while she took the rest of the children back to the living room.

I tried and tried but I couldn't lift Ralph. He must weigh a ton. So I left him sleeping on Fudge's floor and closed the door so he wouldn't hear any noise. On my way back to the living room I wished the others would fall asleep too.

"Peter," my mother suggested, "why don't you show them Dribble?"

"Mom! Dribble's my pet." You don't go around using a pet to entertain a bunch of little kids. Didn't my mother know that?

"Please, Peter," my mother said. "We've still got half an hour left and I don't know what to do with them anymore."

"Dribble!" Fudge hollered. "Dribble . . . Dribble . . . Dribble!"

I guess Sam and Jennie liked the way that sounded because they started to shout, "Dribble . . . Dribble . . . Dribble!" even though they didn't know what they were talking about.

"Oh . . . all right," I said. "I'll show you Dribble. But you've got to promise to be very quiet. You mustn't make a sound. You might scare him . . . okay?"

They all said "Okay." My mother went into the kitchen to chat with Grandma and Mrs. Rudder. I went into my room and came back carrying Dribble in his bowl. I put my finger over my lips to remind Fudge and his friends to be quiet. It worked. At first nobody said a word.

I put Dribble down on a table. Fudge and Sam and Jennie stood over his bowl.

"Oh . . . turtle!" Jennie said.

"Yes, Dribble's a turtle. *My* turtle," I said in a soft voice.

"See . . . see," Fudge whispered.

"They can all see," I told Fudge.

"Nice turtle," Sam said.

I wondered why he wasn't afraid this time.

"What does Dribble do?" Jennie asked.

"Do? He doesn't do anything special," I said. "He's a turtle. He does turtle things."

"Like what?" Jennie asked.

What was with this kid, anyway? "Well," I said, "he swims around a little and he sleeps on his rock and he eats."

"Does he make?" Jennie asked.

"Make?" I said.

"Make a tinkle?"

"Oh, that. Well, sure. I guess so."

Jennie laughed. So did Sam and Fudge.

"I make tinkles too. Want to see?" Jennie asked.

"No," I said.

"See . . . see," Fudge laughed, pointing at Jennie.

Jennie had a big smile on her face. Next thing I knew there was a puddle on the rug.

"Mom!" I hollered. "Come quick!"

My mother dashed in from the kitchen. "What, Peter? What is it?"

"Just look at what Jennie did," I said.

"What is that?" my mother asked, eyeing the puddle.

"She made on the floor," I said. "And on purpose!"

"Oh, Jennie!" my mother cried. "You didn't!"

"Did too," Jennie said.

"That was very naughty!" my mother told her. "You come with me." She scooped up Jennie and carried her into the bathroom.

After that Mom mopped up the puddle.

Finally the doorbell rang. It was two-thirty. The party was over. I could hardly believe it. I was beginning to think it would never end.

First Ralph's mother came. She had to wake him up to

get him out of the apartment. I guess even *she* couldn't carry him.

Next Jennie's mother came. Mom gave her Jennie's wet pants in a Baggie. That was all she had to do. Jennie's mother was plenty embarrassed.

Sam's mother came last. But he didn't want to go home. Now that he was used to us I guess he liked us. He cried, "More party . . . MORE!"

"Another time," his mother said, dragging him out of our apartment by the arm.

My mother flopped down in a chair. Grandma brought her two aspirins and a glass of water. "Here, dear," she said. "Maybe these will help."

My mother swallowed the pills. She held her head.

"Three is kind of young for a party," I told my mother.

"Peter Warren Hatcher . . ." my mother began.

"Yes?" I asked.

"You are absolutely right!"

I flopped down next to my mother. She put her arm around me. Then we both watched Fudge work his new jack-in-the-box.

Later, when my father came home, he said, "How did Fudge's party go?"

My mother and I looked at each other and we laughed.

# Homer Price

from *Homer Price* by Robert McCloskey

**THE VIKING PRESS, 1943**

# About Homer Price

"Where did you get that crazy idea?" a child once asked Robert McCloskey about Homer's adventure with his uncle's amazing automatic doughnut machine. "The Doughnuts" was inspired—as were many of the stories McCloskey wrote and illustrated—by memories of his childhood. Once on a boyhood camping trip, McCloskey was following the recipe for fried doughnuts in a lumberjack's cookbook. Sure that the recipe wouldn't make enough, the enterprising young man doubled the ingredients. Little did he know that doughnut batter increases in size as it cooks! McCloskey also had, like his character Uncle Ulysses, "advanced ideas and a weakness for labor saving devices." One of McCloskey's childhood obsessions was inventing: "I collected old electric motors and bits of wire, old clocks and Meccano sets. I built trains and cranes with remote controls, my family's Christmas trees revolved, lights flashed and buzzers buzzed, fuses blew and sparks flew!"

**Robert McCloskey** was born in Hamilton, Ohio, the town that served as the model for *Lentil*, the first of over fourteen books that he wrote and/or illustrated for children. His second book, *Make Way for Ducklings*, won the Caldecott Medal for the most distinguished American picture book for children. *Time of Wonder*, his first book in full color, won him a second Caldecott Medal in 1958, making McCloskey the first artist to receive this honor twice.

## *Meet Homer Price*

About two miles outside of Centerburg where route 56 meets route 56A there lives a boy named Homer. Homer's father owns a tourist camp. Homer's mother cooks fried chicken and hamburgers in the lunch room and takes care of the tourist cabins while his father takes care of the filling station. Homer does odd jobs about the place. Sometimes he washes windshields of cars to help his father, and sometimes he sweeps out cabins or takes care of the lunch room to help his mother.

# The Doughnuts

One Friday night in November Homer overheard his mother talking on the telephone to Aunt Agnes over in Centerburg. "I'll stop by with the car in about half an hour and we can go to the meeting together," she said, because tonight was the night the Ladies' Club was meeting to discuss plans for a box social and to knit and sew for the Red Cross.

"I think I'll come along and keep Uncle Ulysses company while you and Aunt Agnes are at the meeting," said Homer.

So after Homer had combed his hair and his mother had looked to see if she had her knitting instructions and the right size needles, they started for town.

Homer's Uncle Ulysses and Aunt Agnes have a very up and coming lunch room over in Centerburg, just across from the court house on the town square. Uncle Ulysses is a man with advanced ideas and a weakness for labor saving devices. He equipped the lunch room with automatic toasters, automatic coffee maker, automatic dish washer, and an automatic doughnut maker. All just the latest thing in labor saving devices. Aunt Agnes would throw up her hands and sigh every time Uncle Ulysses bought a new labor saving device. Sometimes she became unkindly disposed toward him for days and days. She was of the opinion that Uncle Ulysses just frittered away his spare time over at the barber shop with the sheriff and the boys, so, what was the good of a labor saving device that gave you more time to fritter?

When Homer and his mother got to Centerburg they stopped at the lunch room, and after Aunt Agnes had come out and said, "My, how that boy does grow!" which was what she always said, she went off with Homer's mother in the car. Homer went into the lunch room and said, "Howdy, Uncle Ulysses!"

"Oh, hello, Homer. You're just in time," said Uncle Ulysses. "I've been going over this automatic doughnut machine, oiling the machinery and cleaning the works . . . wonderful things, these labor saving devices."

"Yep," agreed Homer, and he picked up a cloth and started polishing the metal trimmings while Uncle Ulysses tinkered with the inside workings.

"Opfwo-oof!!" sighed Uncle Ulysses and, "Look here, Homer, you've got a mechanical mind. See if you can find

where these two pieces fit in. I'm going across to the barber shop for a spell, 'cause there's somethin' I've got to talk to the sheriff about. There won't be much business here until the double feature is over and I'll be back before then."

Then as Uncle Ulysses went out the door he said, "Uh, Homer, after you get the pieces in place, would you mind mixing up a batch of doughnut batter and putting it in the machine? You could turn the switch and make a few doughnuts to have on hand for the crowd after the movie . . . if you don't mind."

"O.K.," said Homer, "I'll take care of everything."

A few minutes later a customer came in and said, "Good evening, Bud."

Homer looked up from putting the last piece in the doughnut machine and said, "Good evening, Sir, what can I do for you?"

"Well, young feller, I'd like a cup o' coffee and some doughnuts," said the customer.

"I'm sorry, Mister, but we won't have any doughnuts for about half an hour, until I can mix some dough and start this machine. I could give you some very fine sugar rolls instead."

"Well, Bud, I'm in no real hurry so I'll just have a cup o' coffee and wait around a bit for the doughnuts. Fresh doughnuts are always worth waiting for is what I always say."

"O.K.," said Homer, and he drew a cup of coffee from Uncle Ulysses' super automatic coffee maker.

"Nice place you've got here," said the customer.

"Oh, yes," replied Homer, "this is a very up and coming lunch room with all the latest improvements."

"Yes," said the stranger, "must be a good business. I'm in business too. A traveling man in outdoor advertising. I'm a sandwich man, Mr. Gabby's my name."

"My name is Homer. I'm glad to meet you, Mr. Gabby. It must be a fine profession, traveling and advertising sandwiches."

"Oh no," said Mr. Gabby, "I don't advertise sandwiches, I just wear any kind of an ad, one sign on front and one sign on behind, this way . . . Like a sandwich. Ya know what I mean?"

"Oh, I see. That must be fun, and you travel too?" asked Homer as he got out the flour and the baking powder.

"Yeah, I ride the rods between jobs, on freight trains, ya know what I mean?"

"Yes, but isn't that dangerous?" asked Homer.

"Of course there's a certain amount a risk, but you take any method a travel these days, it's all dangerous. Ya know what I mean? Now take airplanes for instance . . . "

Just then a large shiny black car stopped in front of the lunch room and a chauffeur helped a lady out of the rear door. They both came inside and the lady smiled at Homer and said, "We've stopped for a light snack. Some doughnuts and coffee would be simply marvelous."

Then Homer said, "I'm sorry, Ma'm, but the doughnuts won't be ready until I make this batter and start Uncle Ulysses' doughnut machine."

"Well now aren't *you* a clever young man to know how to make *doughnuts!*"

"Well," blushed Homer, "I've really never done it before but I've got a receipt to follow."

"Now, young man, you simply must allow me to help. You know, I haven't made doughnuts for years, but I know the best receipt for doughnuts. It's marvelous, and we really must use it."

"But, Ma'm . . . " said Homer.

"Now just *wait* till you taste these doughnuts," said the lady. "Do you have an apron?" she asked, as she took off her fur coat and her rings and her jewelry and rolled up her sleeves. "Charles," she said to the chauffeur, "hand me that baking powder, that's right, and, young man, we'll need some nutmeg."

So Homer and the chauffeur stood by and handed

things and cracked the eggs while the lady mixed and stirred. Mr. Gabby sat on his stool, sipped his coffee, and looked on with great interest.

"There!" said the lady when all of the ingredients were mixed. "Just *wait* till you taste these doughnuts!"

"It looks like an awful lot of batter," said Homer as he stood on a chair and poured it into the doughnut machine with the help of the chauffeur. "It's about *ten* times as much as Uncle Ulysses ever makes."

"But wait till you taste them!" said the lady with an eager look and a smile.

Homer got down from the chair and pushed a button on the machine marked "*Start.*" Rings of batter started dropping into the hot fat. After a ring of batter was cooked on one side an automatic gadget turned it over and the other side would cook. Then another automatic gadget gave the doughnut a little push and it rolled neatly down a little chute, all ready to eat.

"That's a simply *fascinating* machine," said the lady as she waited for the first doughnut to roll out.

"Here, young man, *you* must have the first one. Now isn't that just *too* delicious!? Isn't it simply marvelous?"

"Yes, Ma'm, it's very good," replied Homer as the lady handed doughnuts to Charles and to Mr. Gabby and asked if they didn't think they were simply divine doughnuts.

"It's an old family receipt!" said the lady with pride.

Homer poured some coffee for the lady and her chauffeur and for Mr. Gabby, and a glass of milk for himself. Then they all sat down at the lunch counter to enjoy another few doughnuts apiece.

"I'm so glad you enjoy my doughnuts," said the lady. "But now, Charles, we really must be going. If you will just take this apron, Homer, and put two dozen doughnuts in a bag to take along, we'll be on our way. And, Charles, don't forget to pay the young man." She rolled down her sleeves and put on her jewelry, then Charles managed to get her into her big fur coat.

"Good night, young man, I haven't had so much fun in years. I *really* haven't!" said the lady, as she went out the door and into the big shiny car.

"Those are sure good doughnuts," said Mr. Gabby as the car moved off.

"You bet!" said Homer. Then he and Mr. Gabby stood and watched the automatic doughnut machine make doughnuts.

After a few dozen more doughnuts had rolled down the little chute, Homer said, "I guess that's about enough doughnuts to sell to the after theater customers. I'd better turn the machine off for a while."

Homer pushed the button marked "*Stop*" and there was a little click, but nothing happened. The rings of batter kept right on dropping into the hot fat, and an automatic gadget kept right on turning them over, and another automatic gadget kept right on giving them a little push and the doughnuts kept right on rolling down the little chute, all ready to eat.

"That's funny," said Homer, "I'm sure that's the right button!" He pushed it again but the automatic doughnut maker kept right on making doughnuts.

"Well I guess I must have put one of those pieces in backwards," said Homer.

"Then it might stop if you pushed the button marked "*Start*," said Mr. Gabby.

Homer did, and the doughnuts still kept rolling down the little chute, just as regular as a clock can tick.

"I guess we could sell a few more doughnuts," said Homer, "but I'd better telephone Uncle Ulysses over at the barber shop." Homer gave the number and while he waited for someone to answer he counted thirty-seven doughnuts roll down the little chute.

Finally someone answered "Hello! This is the sarber bhop, I mean the barber shop."

"Oh, hello, sheriff. This is Homer. Could I speak to Uncle Ulysses?"

"Well, he's playing pinochle right now," said the sheriff. "Anythin' I can tell 'im?"

"Yes," said Homer. "I pushed the button marked *Stop* on the doughnut machine but the rings of batter keep right on dropping into the hot fat, and an automatic gadget keeps right on turning them over, and another automatic gadget keeps giving them a little push, and the doughnuts keep right on rolling down the little chute! It won't stop!"

"O.K. Wold the hire, I mean, hold the wire and I'll tell 'im." Then Homer looked over his shoulder and counted another twenty-one doughnuts roll down the little chute, all ready to eat. Then the sheriff said, "He'll be right over. . . . Just gotta finish this hand."

"That's good," said Homer. "G'by, sheriff."

The window was full of doughnuts by now so Homer and Mr. Gabby had to hustle around and start stacking them on plates and trays and lining them up on the counter.

"Sure are a lot of doughnuts!" said Homer.

"You bet!" said Mr. Gabby. "I lost count at twelve hundred and two and that was quite a while back."

People had begun to gather outside the lunch room window, and someone was saying, "There are almost as many doughnuts as there are people in Centerburg, and I wonder how in tarnation Ulysses thinks he can sell all of 'em!"

Every once in a while somebody would come inside and buy some, but while somebody bought two to eat and a dozen to take home, the machine made three dozen more.

By the time Uncle Ulysses and the sheriff arrived and

pushed through the crowd, the lunch room was a calamity
of doughnuts! Doughnuts in the window, doughnuts piled
high on the shelves, doughnuts stacked on plates, doughnuts lined up twelve deep all along the counter, and dough-

nuts still rolling down the little chute, just as regular as a clock can tick.

"Hello, sheriff, hello, Uncle Ulysses, we're having a little trouble here," said Homer.

"Well, I'll be dunked!!" said Uncle Ulysses.

"Dernd ef you won't be when Aggy gits home," said the sheriff.

"Mighty fine doughnuts though. What'll you do with 'em all, Ulysses?"

Uncle Ulysses groaned and said, "What will Aggy say? We'll never sell 'em all."

Then Mr. Gabby, who hadn't said anything for a long time, stopped piling doughnuts and said, "What you need is an advertising man. Ya know what I mean? You got the doughnuts, ya gotta create a market . . . Understand? . . . It's balancing the demand with the supply . . . That sort of thing."

"Yep!" said Homer. "Mr. Gabby's right. We have to enlarge our market. He's an advertising sandwich man, so if we hire him, he can walk up and down in front of the theater and get the customers."

"You're hired, Mr. Gabby!" said Uncle Ulysses.

Then everybody pitched in to paint the signs and to get Mr. Gabby sandwiched between. They painted "SALE ON DOUGHNUTS" in big letters on the window too.

Meanwhile the rings of batter kept right on dropping into the hot fat, and an automatic gadget kept right on turning them over, and another automatic gadget kept right on giving them a little push, and the doughnuts kept right on rolling down the little chute, just as regular as a clock can tick.

"I certainly hope this advertising works," said Uncle Ulysses, wagging his head. "Aggy'll certainly throw a fit if it don't."

The sheriff went outside to keep order, because there was quite a crowd by now—all looking at the doughnuts and guessing how many thousand there were, and watching new ones roll down the little chute, just as regular as a clock can tick. Homer and Uncle Ulysses kept stacking doughnuts. Once in a while somebody bought a few, but not very often.

Then Mr. Gabby came back and said, "Say, you know there's not much use o' me advertisin' at the theater. The show's all over, and besides almost everybody in town is out front watching that machine make doughnuts!"

"Zeus!" said Uncle Ulysses. "We must get rid of these doughnuts before Aggy gets here!"

"Looks like you will have ta hire a truck ta waul 'em ahay, I mean haul 'em away!!" said the sheriff who had just come in. Just then there was a noise and a shoving out front and the lady from the shiny black car and her chauffeur came pushing through the crowd and into the lunch room.

"Oh, gracious!" she gasped, ignoring the doughnuts, "I've lost my diamond bracelet, and I know I left it here on the counter," she said, pointing to a place where the doughnuts were piled in stacks of two dozen.

"Yes, Ma'm, I guess you forgot it when you helped make the batter," said Homer.

Then they moved all the doughnuts around and looked for the diamond bracelet, but they couldn't find it anywhere. Meanwhile the doughnuts kept rolling down the little chute, just as regular as a clock can tick.

After they had looked all around the sheriff cast a suspicious eye on Mr. Gabby, but Homer said, "He's all right, sheriff, he didn't take it. He's a friend of mine."

Then the lady said, "I'll offer a reward of one hundred dollars for that bracelet! It really *must* be found! . . . it *really* must!"

"Now don't you worry, lady," said the sheriff. "I'll get your bracelet back!"

"Zeus! This is terrible!" said Uncle Ulysses. "First all of these doughnuts and then on top of all that, a lost diamond bracelet . . ."

Mr. Gabby tried to comfort him, and he said, "There's always a bright side. That machine'll probably run outta batter in an hour or two."

If Mr. Gabby hadn't been quick on his feet Uncle Ulysses would have knocked him down, sure as fate.

Then while the lady wrung her hands and said, "We must find it, we *must*!" and Uncle Ulysses was moaning about what Aunt Agnes would say, and the sheriff was

eyeing Mr. Gabby, Homer sat down and thought hard.

Before twenty more doughnuts could roll down the little chute he shouted, "SAY! I know where the bracelet is! It was lying here on the counter and got mixed up in the batter by mistake! The bracelet is cooked inside one of these doughnuts!"

"Why . . . I really believe you're right," said the lady through her tears. "Isn't that *amazing*? Simply *amazing*!"

"I'll be durn'd!" said the sheriff.

"OhH-h!" moaned Uncle Ulysses. "Now we have to break up all of these doughnuts to find it. Think of the *pieces!* Think of the *crumbs!* Think of what *Aggy* will say!"

"Nope," said Homer. "We won't have to break them up. I've got a plan."

So Homer and the advertising man took some cardboard and some paint and printed another sign. They put this sign in the window, and the sandwich man wore two more signs that said the same thing and walked around in the crowd out front.

THEN . . . The doughnuts began to sell! *Everybody* wanted to buy doughnuts, *dozens* of doughnuts!

And that's not all. Everybody bought coffee to dunk the doughnuts in too. Those that didn't buy coffee bought milk or soda. It kept Homer and the lady and the chauffeur and Uncle Ulysses and the sheriff busy waiting on the people who wanted to buy doughnuts.

When all but the last couple of hundred doughnuts had been sold, Rupert Black shouted, "I GAWT IT!!" and sure enough . . . there was the diamond bracelet inside of his doughnut!

Then Rupert went home with a hundred dollars, the citizens of Centerburg went home full of doughnuts, the lady and her chauffeur drove off with the diamond bracelet, and Homer went home with his mother when she stopped by with Aunt Aggy.

As Homer went out of the door he heard Mr. Gabby say, "Neatest trick of merchandising I ever seen," and Aunt Aggy was looking sceptical while Uncle Ulysses was saying, "The rings of batter kept right on dropping into the hot fat, and the automatic gadget kept right on turning them over, and the other automatic gadget kept right on giving them a little push, and the doughnuts kept right on rolling down the little chute just as regular as a clock can tick—they just kept right on a comin', an' a comin, an' a comin', an' a comin'."

# Sam Gribley

from *My Side of the Mountain* by Jean Craighead George
**E. P. DUTTON, 1959**

# About Sam Gribley

When she was in elementary school, Jean Craighead George packed her suitcase and told her mother she was going to run away from home. As she envisioned it, she would live by a waterfall in the woods and catch fish on hooks made from the forks of tree limbs, as she had been taught by her father. Wisely, her mother did not try to dissuade her. She checked her daughter's bag to see if she had her toothbrush and kissed her good-bye. Forty minutes later, the girl was home.

Jean Craighead George's love of nature has been the inspiration for her more than forty books for young people. George's father, a naturalist and scientist, taught her the plants and animals of eastern forests. Her brothers, two of the first licensed falconers in the United States, helped her in the training of a falcon.

George remembered a huge tree her brothers had camped in on an island in the Potomac River. In her mind, this tree would be Sam Gribley's home as he found ways to survive in the Catskill Mountains. The first draft of *My Side of the Mountain* was done in two weeks.

*My Side of the Mountain* was first published in the spring of 1959, and has been translated into many languages. It is a Newbery Honor Book, an ALA Notable Book, and a Hans Christian Andersen Award Honor Book. Known and loved by readers around the world, it was described by *The Horn Book* as "extraordinary. . . . It will be read year after year, linking together many generations in a chain of well-remembered joy and refreshment." The novel was also made into a major motion picture in 1968 by Paramount Pictures Corp.

**Jean Craighead George** was born in 1919 and raised in Washington, D.C. She graduated from Pennsylvania State University and three years later married John L. George. They then began a joint career writing and illustrating nature books. They have three children. Now divorced, Mrs. George has continued to write outstanding nature books. *Julie of the Wolves,* one of the many beloved books she has written and/or illustrated for young people, won the Newbery Medal in 1973. Jean Craighead George lives and writes in Chappaqua, New York.

# In Which I Hole Up
# in a Snowstorm

I am on my mountain in a tree home that people have passed without ever knowing that I am here. The house is a hemlock tree six feet in diameter, and must be as old as the mountain itself. I came upon it last summer and dug and burned it out until I made a snug cave in the tree that I now call home.

"My bed is on the right as you enter, and is made of ash slats and covered with deerskin. On the left is a small fireplace about knee high. It is of clay and stones. It has a chimney that leads the smoke out through a knothole. I chipped out three other knotholes to let fresh air in. The air coming in is bitter cold. It must be below zero outside, and yet I can sit here inside my tree and write with bare hands. The fire is small, too. It doesn't take much fire to warm this tree room.

"It is the fourth of December, I think. It may be the fifth. I am not sure because I have not recently counted the notches in the aspen pole that is my calendar. I have been just too busy gathering nuts and berries, smoking venison, fish, and small game to keep up with the exact date.

"The lamp I am writing by is deer fat poured into a turtle shell with a strip of my old city trousers for a wick.

"It snowed all day yesterday and today. I have not been outside since the storm began, and I am bored for the first time since I ran away from home eight months ago to live on the land.

"I am well and healthy. The food is good. Sometimes I eat turtle soup, and I know how to make acorn pancakes. I keep my supplies in the wall of the tree in wooden pockets that I chopped myself.

"Every time I have looked at those pockets during the last two days, I have felt just like a squirrel, which reminds me: I didn't see a squirrel one whole day before that storm began. I guess they are holed up and eating their stored nuts, too.

"I wonder if The Baron, that's the wild weasel who lives behind the big boulder to the north of my tree, is also denned up. Well, anyway, I think the storm is dying down because the tree is not crying so much. When the wind really blows, the whole tree moans right down to the roots, which is where I am.

"Tomorrow I hope The Baron and I can tunnel out into the sunlight. I wonder if I should dig the snow. But that would mean I would have to put it somewhere, and the only place to put it is in my nice snug tree. Maybe I can pack it with my hands as I go. I've always dug into the snow from the top, never up from under.

"The Baron must dig up from under the snow. I wonder where he puts what he digs? Well, I guess I'll know in the morning."

When I wrote that last winter, I was scared and thought maybe I'd never get out of my tree. I had been scared for two days—ever since the first blizzard hit the Catskill Mountains. When I came up to the sunlight, which I did by simply poking my head into the soft snow and standing up, I laughed at my dark fears.

Everything was white, clean, shining, and beautiful. The sky was blue, blue, blue. The hemlock grove was laced with snow, the meadow was smooth and white, and the gorge was sparkling with ice. It was so beautiful and peaceful that I laughed out loud. I guess I laughed because my first snowstorm was over and it had not been so terrible after all.

Then I shouted, "I did it!" My voice never got very far. It was hushed by the tons of snow.

I looked for signs from The Baron Weasel. His footsteps were all over the boulder, also slides where he had played. He must have been up for hours, enjoying the new snow.

Inspired by his fun, I poked my head into my tree and whistled. Frightful, my trained falcon, flew to my fist, and we jumped and slid down the mountain, making big holes and trenches as we went. It was good to be whistling and carefree again, because I was sure scared by the coming of that storm.

I had been working since May, learning how to make a fire with flint and steel, finding what plants I could eat, how to trap animals and catch fish—all this so that when the curtain of blizzard struck the Catskills, I could crawl inside my tree and be comfortably warm and have plenty to eat.

During the summer and fall I had thought about the coming of winter. However, on that third day of December when the sky blackened, the temperature dropped, and the first flakes swirled around me, I must admit that I wanted to run back to New York. Even the first night that I spent out in the woods, when I couldn't get the fire started, was not as frightening as the snowstorm that gathered behind the gorge and mushroomed up over my mountain.

I was smoking three trout. It was nine o'clock in the morning. I was busy keeping the flames low so they would not leap up and burn the fish. As I worked, it occurred to me that it was awfully dark for that hour of the morning. Frightful was leashed to her tree stub. She seemed restless and pulled at her tethers. Then I realized that the forest was dead quiet. Even the woodpeckers that had been tapping around me all morning were silent. The squirrels were nowhere to be seen. The juncos and chickadees and nuthatches were gone. I looked to see what The Baron Weasel was doing. He was not around. I looked up.

From my tree you can see the gorge beyond the meadow. White water pours between the black wet boulders and cascades into the valley below. The water that day was as dark as the rocks. Only the sound told me it was still falling. Above the darkness stood another darkness. The clouds of winter, black and fearsome. They looked as wild as the winds that were bringing them. I grew sick with fright. I knew I had enough food. I knew everything was going to be perfectly all right. But knowing that didn't help. I was scared. I stamped out the fire and pocketed the fish.

I tried to whistle for Frightful, but couldn't purse my shaking lips tight enough to get out anything but *pfffff.* So I grabbed her by the hide straps that are attached to her legs and we dove through the deerskin door into my room in the tree.

I put Frightful on the bedpost, and curled up in a ball on the bed. I thought about New York and the noise and the lights and how a snowstorm always seemed very friendly there. I thought about our apartment, too. At that moment it seemed bright and lighted and warm. I had to keep saying to myself: There were eleven of us in it! Dad, Mother, four sisters, four brothers, and me. And not one of us liked it, except perhaps little Nina, who was too young to know. Dad didn't like it even a little bit. He had been a sailor once, but when I was born, he gave up the sea and worked on the docks in New York. Dad didn't like the land. He liked the sea, wet and big and endless.

Sometimes he would tell me about Great-grandfather Gribley, who owned land in the Catskill Mountains and felled the trees and built a home and plowed the land—only to discover that he wanted to be a sailor. The farm failed, and Great-grandfather Gribley went to sea.

As I lay with my face buried in the sweet greasy smell of my deerskin, I could hear Dad's voice saying, "That land is still in the family's name. Somewhere in the Catskills is an old beech with the name *Gribley* carved on it. It marks the northern boundary of Gribley's folly—the land is no place for a Gribley."

"The land is no place for a Gribley," I said. "The land is no place for a Gribley, and here I am three hundred feet from the beech with *Gribley* carved on it."

I fell asleep at that point, and when I awoke I was hungry. I cracked some walnuts, got down the acorn flour I had pounded, with a bit of ash to remove the bite, reached out the door for a little snow, and stirred up some acorn pancakes. I cooked them on a top of a tin can, and as I ate them, smothered with blueberry jam, I knew that the land was just the place for a Gribley.

# In Which I Get
# Started on This Venture

I left New York in May. I had a penknife, a ball of cord, an ax, and $40, which I had saved from selling magazine subscriptions. I also had some flint and steel which I had bought at a Chinese store in the city. The man in the store had showed me how to use it. He had also given me a little purse to put it in, and some tinder to catch the sparks. He had told me that if I ran out of tinder, I should burn cloth, and use the charred ashes.

I thanked him and said, "This is the kind of thing I am not going to forget."

On the train north to the Catskills I unwrapped my flint and steel and practiced hitting them together to make sparks. On the wrapping paper I made these notes.

"A hard brisk strike is best. Remember to hold the steel in the left hand and the flint in the right, and hit the steel with the flint.
"The trouble is the sparks go every which way."

And that *was* the trouble. I did not get a fire going that night, and as I mentioned, this was a scary experience.

I hitched rides into the Catskill Mountains. At about four o'clock a truck driver and I passed through a beautiful dark hemlock forest, and I said to him, "This is as far as I am going."

He looked all around and said, "You live here?"

"No," I said, "but I am running away from home, and this is just the kind of forest I have always dreamed I would run to. I think I'll camp here tonight." I hopped out of the cab.

"Hey, boy," the driver shouted. "Are you serious?"

"Sure," I said.

"Well, now, ain't that sumpin'? You know, when I was your age, I did the same thing. Only thing was, I was a farm boy and ran to the city, and you're a city boy running to the woods. I was scared of the city—do you think you'll be scared of the woods?"

"Heck, no!" I shouted loudly.

As I marched into the cool shadowy woods, I heard the driver call to me, "I'll be back in the morning, if you want to ride home."

He laughed. Everybody laughed at me. Even Dad. I told Dad that I was going to run away to Great-grandfather Gribley's land. He had roared with laughter and told me about the time he had run away from home. He got on a boat headed for Singapore, but when the whistle blew for departure, he was down the gangplank and home in bed before anyone knew he was gone. Then he told me, "Sure, go try it. Every boy should try it."

I must have walked a mile into the woods until I found a stream. It was a clear athletic stream that rushed and ran and jumped and splashed. Ferns grew along its bank, and its rocks were upholstered with moss.

I sat down, smelled the piney air, and took out my penknife. I cut off a green twig and began to whittle. I have always been good at whittling. I carved a ship once that my teacher exhibited for parents' night at school.

First I whittled an angle on one end of the twig. Then I cut

a smaller twig and sharpened it to a point. I whittled an angle on
that twig, and bound the two angles face to face with a strip of
green bark. It was supposed to be a fishhook.

According to a book on how to survive on the land that I
read in the New York Public Library, this was the way to make

sharpen

whittle angles      string

wooden fishhook

your own hooks. I then dug for worms. I had hardly chopped
the moss away with my ax before I hit frost. It had not occurred
to me that there would be frost in the ground in May, but then,
I had not been on a mountain before.

This did worry me, because I was depending on fish to
keep me alive until I got to my great-grandfather's mountain,
where I was going to make traps and catch game.

I looked into the stream to see what else I could eat, and as
I did, my hand knocked a rotten log apart. I remembered about
old logs and all the sleeping stages of insects that are in it. I
chopped away until I found a cold white grub.

I swiftly tied a string to my hook, put the grub on, and
walked up the stream looking for a good place to fish. All the
manuals I had read were very emphatic about where fish lived,
and so I had memorized this: "In streams, fish usually congre-
gate in pools and deep calm water. The heads of riffles, small
rapids, the tail of a pool, eddies below rocks or logs, deep undercut banks, in the shade of overhanging bushes—all are very likely
places to fish."

This stream did not seem to have any calm water, and I must have walked a thousand miles before I found a pool by a deep undercut bank in the shade of overhanging bushes. Actually, it wasn't that far, it just seemed that way because as I went looking and finding nothing, I was sure I was going to starve to death.

I squatted on this bank and dropped in my line. I did so want to catch a fish. One fish would set me upon my way, because I had read how much you can learn from one fish. By examining the contents of its stomach you can find what the other fish are eating or you can use the internal organs as bait.

The grub went down to the bottom of the stream. It swirled around and hung still. Suddenly the string came to life, and rode back and forth and around in a circle. I pulled with a powerful jerk. The hook came apart, and whatever I had went circling back to its bed.

Well, that almost made me cry. My bait was gone, my hook was broken, and I was getting cold, frightened, and mad. I whittled another hook, but this time I cheated and used string to wind it together instead of bark. I walked back to the log and luckily found another grub. I hurried to the pool, and flipped a trout out of the water before I knew I had a bite.

The fish flopped, and I threw my whole body over it. I could not bear to think of it flopping itself back into the stream.

I cleaned it like I had seen the man at the fish market do, examined its stomach, and found it empty. This horrified me. What I didn't know was that an empty stomach means the fish are hungry and will eat about anything. However, I thought at the time that I was a goner. Sadly, I put some of the internal organs on my hook, and before I could get my line to the bottom I had another bite. I lost that one, but got the next one. I stopped when I had five nice little trout and looked around for a place to build a camp and make a fire.

It wasn't hard to find a pretty spot along that stream. I selected a place beside a mossy rock in a circle of hemlocks.

I decided to make a bed before I cooked. I cut off some boughs for a mattress, then I leaned some dead limbs against the boulder and covered them with hemlock limbs. This made a kind of tent. I crawled in, lay down, and felt alone and secret and very excited.

But ah, the rest of this story! I was on the northeast side of the mountain. It grew dark and cold early. Seeing the shadows slide down on me, I frantically ran around gathering firewood. This is about the only thing I did right from that moment until dawn, because I remembered that the driest wood in a forest is the dead limbs that are still on the trees, and I gathered an enormous pile of them. That pile must still be there, for I never got a fire going.

I got sparks, sparks, sparks. I even hit the tinder with the sparks. The tinder burned all right, but that was as far as I got.

I blew on it, I breathed on it, I cupped it in my hands, but no sooner did I add twigs than the whole thing went black.

Then it got too dark to see. I clicked steel and flint together, even though I couldn't see the tinder. Finally, I gave up and crawled into my hemlock tent, hungry, cold, and miserable.

I can talk about that first night now, although it is still embarrassing to me because I was so stupid, and scared, that I hate to admit it.

I had made my hemlock bed right in the stream valley where the wind drained down from the cold mountaintop. It might have been all right if I had made it on the other side of the boulder, but I didn't. I was right on the main highway of the cold winds as they tore down upon the valley below. I didn't have enough hemlock boughs under me, and before I had my head down, my stomach was cold and damp. I took some boughs off the roof and stuffed them under me, and then my shoulders were cold. I curled up in a ball and was almost asleep when a whippoorwill called. If you have ever been within forty feet of a whippoorwill, you will understand why I couldn't even shut my eyes. They are deafening!

Well, anyway, the whole night went like that. I don't think I slept fifteen minutes, and I was so scared and tired that my throat was dry. I wanted a drink but didn't dare go near the stream for fear of making a misstep and falling in and getting wet. So I sat tight, and shivered and shook—and now I am able to say—I cried a little tiny bit.

Fortunately, the sun has a wonderfully glorious habit of rising every morning. When the sky lightened, when the birds awoke, I knew I would never again see anything so splendid as the round red sun coming up over the earth.

*a couple of good shelters - make sure your fire is on scraped earth - also be sure to put it out!*

I was immediately cheered, and set out directly for the highway. Somehow, I thought that if I was a little nearer the road, everything would be all right.

I climbed a hill and stopped. There was a house. A house warm and cozy, with smoke coming out the chimney and lights in the windows, and only a hundred feet from my torture camp.

Without considering my pride, I ran down the hill and banged on the door. A nice old man answered. I told him everything in one long sentence, and then said, "And so, can I cook my fish here, because I haven't eaten in years."

He chuckled, stroked his whiskery face, and took the fish. He had them cooking in a pan before I knew what his name was.

When I asked him, he said Bill something, but I never heard his last name because I fell asleep in his rocking chair that was pulled up beside his big hot glorious wood stove in the kitchen.

I ate the fish some hours later, also some bread, jelly, oatmeal, and cream. Then he said to me, "Sam Gribley, if you are going to run off and live in the woods, you better learn how to make a fire. Come with me."

We spent the afternoon practicing. I penciled these notes on the back of a scrap of paper, so I wouldn't forget.

"When the tinder glows, keep blowing and add fine dry needles one by one—and keep blowing, steadily, lightly, and evenly. Add one inch dry twigs to the needles and then give her a good big handful of small dry stuff. Keep blowing."

# The Manner in Which
# I Find Gribley's Farm

The next day I told Bill good-by, and as I strode, warm and fed, onto the road, he called to me, "I'll see you tonight. The back door will be open if you want a roof over your head."

I said, "Okay," but I knew I wouldn't see Bill again. I knew how to make fire, and that was my weapon. With fire I could conquer the Catskills. I also knew how to fish. To fish and to make a fire. That was all I needed to know, I thought.

Three rides that morning took me to Delhi. Somewhere around here was Great-grandfather's beech tree with the name *Gribley* carved on it. This much I knew from Dad's stories.

By six o'clock I still had not found anyone who had even heard of the Gribleys, much less Gribley's beech, and so I slept on the porch of a schoolhouse and ate chocolate bars for supper. It was cold and hard, but I was so tired I could have slept in a wind tunnel.

At dawn I thought real hard: Where would I find out about the Gribley farm? Some old map, I said. Where would I find an old map? The library? Maybe. I'd try it and see.

The librarian was very helpful. She was sort of young, had brown hair and brown eyes, and loved books as much as I did.

The library didn't open until ten-thirty. I got there at nine. After I had lolled and rolled and sat on the steps for fifteen or twenty minutes, the door whisked open, and this tall lady asked me to come on in and browse around until opening time.

All I said to her was that I wanted to find the old Gribley

farm, and that the Gribleys hadn't lived on it for maybe a hundred years, and she was off. I can still hear her heels click, when I think of her, scattering herself around those shelves finding me old maps, histories of the Catskills, and files of letters and deeds that must have come from attics around Delhi.

Miss Turner—that was her name—found it. She found Gribley's farm in an old book of Delaware County. Then she worked out the roads to it, and drew me maps and everything. Finally she said, "What do you want to know for? Some school project?"

"Oh, no, Miss Turner, I want to go live there."

# Pippi
# Longstocking

from *Pippi Longstocking* by Astrid Lindgren,
illustrated by Michael Chesworth in 1997
**THE VIKING PRESS, 1950**

# About Pippi Longstocking

Astrid Lindgren is often asked how she came to write about Pippi Longstocking. "In 1941, my seven-year-old daughter, Karin, was sick in bed with pneumonia, and one evening she asked me to tell her a story about 'Pippi Longstocking.' I didn't ask her who Pippi Longstocking was, I just began the story, and since it was a strange name it turned out to be a strange girl as well." A few years later, when Astrid Lindgren was recuperating from a sprained ankle, she wrote the stories down. When she sent the manuscript to a publisher two years later, she knew it was an unorthodox subject for a children's book, and added the note "In the hope that you won't notify the Child Welfare Committee!"

**Astrid Lindgren** was born in 1907 and spent an idyllic childhood on a farm in Sweden with her brother and two sisters. The many games and pranks they played together, and especially the love of nature that was to last throughout Lindgren's life, inform all her work. By far the most famous and popular author in Sweden, Astrid Lindgren is also involved in political causes, and the 1987 Swedish Animal Rights Reform Law is popularly known as "Lex Lindgren." Among the many honors and prizes awarded to Lindgren is the 1958 Hans Christian Andersen Medal for her contribution to international children's literature. When an interviewer once commented that Pippi Longstocking is a character that seems to have always been around, Ms. Lindgren replied, "Maybe she was just waiting for someone to pick her up and write about her."

# Pippi Moves into Villa Villekulla

**W**ay out at the end of a tiny little town was an old over-grown garden, and in the garden was an old house, and in the house lived Pippi Longstocking. She was nine years old, and she lived there all alone. She had no mother and no father, and that was of course very nice because there was no one to tell her to go to bed just when she was having the most fun, and no one who could make her take cod liver oil when she much preferred caramel candy.

Her father had bought the old house in the garden many years ago. He thought he would live there with Pippi when he grew old and couldn't sail the seas any longer. And then this annoying thing had to happen, that he was blown into the ocean, and while Pippi was waiting for him to come back she went straight home to Villa Villekulla. That was the name of the house. It stood there ready and waiting for her. One lovely summer evening she had said good-by to all the sailors on her father's boat. They were all fond of Pippi, and she of them.

Two things she took with her from the ship: a little monkey whose name was Mr. Nilsson—he was a present from her father—and a big suitcase full of gold pieces.

Pippi was a remarkable child. The most remarkable thing about her was that she was so strong. She was so very strong that in the whole wide world there was not a single police officer as strong as she. Why, she could lift a whole horse if she wanted to! And she wanted to. She had a horse of her own that she had bought with one of her many gold pieces the day she came home to Villa Villekulla. She had always longed for a horse, and now here he was, living on the porch. When Pippi wanted to drink her afternoon coffee there, she simply lifted him down into the garden.

Beside Villa Villekulla was another garden and another house. In that house lived a father and mother and two charming children, a boy and a girl. The boy's name was Tommy and the girl's Annika. Tommy and Annika played nicely with each other in their garden, but they had often wished for a playmate. While Pippi was still sailing the ocean with her father, they often used to hang over the fence and say to each other, "Isn't it silly that nobody ever moves into that house. Somebody ought to live there—somebody with children."

On that lovely summer evening when Pippi for the first time stepped over the threshold of Villa Villekulla, Tommy and Annika were not at home—they had no idea that anybody had moved into the house next door. On the first day after they came home again they stood by the gate, looking out onto the street, and even then they didn't know that there actually was a playmate so near. Just as they were standing there considering what they should do and wondering whether anything exciting was likely to happen or whether it was going to be one of those dull days when they couldn't think of anything to play—just then the gate of Villa Villekulla opened and a little girl stepped out. She was the most remarkable girl Tommy and Annika had ever seen. She was Miss Pippi Longstocking out for her morning promenade. This is the way she looked:

Her hair, the color of a carrot, was braided in two tight braids that stuck straight out. Her nose was the shape of a very small potato and was dotted all over with freckles. It must be

admitted that the mouth under this nose was a very wide one, with strong white teeth. Her dress was rather unusual. Pippi herself had made it. She had meant it to be blue, but there wasn't quite enough blue cloth, so Pippi had sewed little red pieces on it here and there. On her long thin legs she wore a pair of long stockings, one brown and the other black, and she had on a pair of black shoes that were exactly twice as long as her feet. These shoes her father had bought for her in South America so that Pippi would have something to grow into, and she never wanted to wear any others.

But the one thing that made Tommy and Annika open their eyes widest of all was the monkey sitting on the strange girl's shoulder. It was a little monkey, dressed in blue pants, yellow jacket, and a white straw hat.

"Do you live here all alone?" Annika said anxiously.

"Of course not!" said Pippi. "Mr. Nilsson and the horse live here too."

"Yes, but I mean don't you have any mother or father here?"

"No, not the least little tiny bit of a one," said Pippi happily.

"But who tells you when to go to bed at night and things like that?" asked Annika.

"I tell myself," said Pippi. "First I tell myself in a nice friendly way; and then, if I don't mind, I tell myself again more sharply; and if I still don't mind, then I'm in for a spanking—see?"

Tommy and Annika didn't see at all, but they thought maybe it was a good way.

# Pippi
# Goes to the Circus

Acircus had come to the little town, and all the children were begging their mothers and fathers for permission to go. Of course Tommy and Annika asked to go too, and their kind father immediately gave them some money.

Clutching it tightly in their hands, they rushed over to Pippi's. She was on the porch with her horse, braiding his tail into tiny pigtails and tying each one with red ribbon.

"I think it's his birthday today," she announced, "so he has to be all dressed up."

"Pippi," said Tommy, all out of breath because they had been running so fast, "Pippi, do you want to go with us to the circus?"

"I can go with you most anywhere," answered Pippi, "but whether I can go to the surkus or not I don't know, because I don't know what a surkus is. Does it hurt?"

"Silly!" said Tommy. "Of course it doesn't hurt; it's fun. Horses and clowns and pretty ladies that walk the tightrope."

"But it costs money," said Annika, opening her small fist to see if the shiny half-dollar and the quarters were still there.

"I'm rich as a troll," said Pippi, "so I guess I can buy a surkus all right. But it'll be crowded here if I have more horses. The clowns and the pretty ladies I could keep in the laundry, but it's harder to know what to do with the horses."

"Oh, don't be so silly," said Tommy, "you don't buy a circus. It costs money to go and look at it—see?"

"Preserve us!" cried Pippi and shut her eyes tightly. "It costs money to *look*? And here I go around goggling all day long. Goodness knows how much money I've goggled up already!"

Then, little by little, she opened one eye very carefully, and it rolled round and round in her head. "Cost what it may," she said, "I must take a look!"

At last Tommy and Annika managed to explain to Pippi what a circus really was, and she took some gold pieces out of her suitcase. Then she put on her hat, which was as big as a millstone, and off they all went.

There were crowds of people outside the circus tent and a long line at the ticket window. But at last it was Pippi's turn. She stuck her head through the window and stared at the dear old lady sitting there.

"How much does it cost to look at you?" Pippi asked.

But the old lady was a foreigner who did not understand what Pippi meant and answered in broken Swedish.

"Little girl, it costs a dollar and a quarter in the grand-stand and seventy-five cents on the benches and twenty-five cents for standing room."

Now Tommy interrupted and said that Pippi wanted a seventy-five-cent ticket. Pippi put down a gold piece and the old lady looked suspiciously at it. She bit it too, to see if it was genuine. At last she was convinced that it really was gold and gave Pippi her ticket and a great deal of change in silver.

"What would I do with all those nasty little white coins?" asked Pippi disgustedly. "Keep them and then I can look at you twice. In the standing room."

As Pippi absolutely refused to accept any change, the lady changed her ticket to one for the grandstand and gave Tommy and Annika grandstand tickets too without their having to pay a single penny. In that way Pippi, Tommy, and Annika came to sit on some beautiful red chairs right next to the ring. Tommy and Annika turned around several times to wave to their schoolmates, who were sitting much farther away.

"This is a remarkable place," said Pippi, looking around in astonishment. "But, see, they've spilled sawdust all over the floor! Not that I'm overfussy myself, but that does look careless to me."

Tommy explained that all circuses had sawdust on the floor for the horses to run around in.

On a platform nearby the circus band suddenly began to play a thundering march. Pippi clapped her hands wildly and jumped up and down with delight.

"Does it cost money to hear too?" she asked. "Or can you do that for nothing?"

At that moment the curtain in front of the performers' entrance was drawn aside, and the ringmaster in a black frock coat, with a whip in his hand, came running in, followed by ten white horses with red plumes on their heads.

The ringmaster cracked his whip, and all the horses galloped around the ring. Then he cracked it again, and all the horses stood still with their front feet up on the railing around the ring.

One of them had stopped directly in front of the children. Annika didn't like to have a horse so near her and drew back in her chair as far as she could, but Pippi leaned forward and took the horse's right foot in her hands.

"Hello, there," she said, "my horse sent you his best wishes. It's his birthday today too, but he has bows on his tail instead of on his head."

Luckily she dropped the foot before the ringmaster cracked his whip again, because then all the horses jumped away from the railing and began to run around the ring.

When the act was over, the ringmaster bowed politely and the horses ran out. In an instant the curtain opened again for a coal-black horse. On its back stood a beautiful lady dressed in green silk tights. The program said her name was Miss Carmencita.

The horse trotted around in the sawdust, and Miss Carmencita stood calmly on his back and smiled. But then something happened; just as the horse passed Pippi's seat, something came swishing through the air—and it was none other than Pippi herself. And there she stood on the horse's back, behind Miss Carmencita. At first Miss Carmencita was so astonished that she nearly fell off the horse. Then she got mad. She began to strike out with her hands behind her back to make Pippi jump off. But that didn't work.

"Take it easy," said Pippi. "Do you think you're the only one who can have any fun? Other people have paid too, haven't they?"

Then Miss Carmencita tried to jump off herself, but that didn't work either, because Pippi was holding her tightly around the waist. At that the audience couldn't help laughing. They thought it was funny to see the lovely Miss Carmencita held against her will by a little red-headed youngster who stood there on the horse's back in her enormous shoes and looked as if she had never done anything except perform in a circus.

But the ringmaster didn't laugh. He turned toward an attendant in a red uniform and made a sign to him to go and stop the horse.

"Is this act already over," asked Pippi in a disappointed tone, "just when we were having so much fun?"

"Horrible child!" hissed the ringmaster between his teeth. "Get out of here!"

Pippi looked at him sadly. "Why are you mad at me?" she asked. "What's the matter? I thought we were here to have fun."

She skipped off the horse and went back to her seat. But now two huge guards came to throw her out. They took hold of her and tried to lift her up.

They couldn't do it. Pippi sat absolutely still, and it was impossible to budge her although they tried as hard as they could. At last they shrugged their shoulders and went off.

Meanwhile the next act had begun. It was Miss Elvira about to walk the tightrope. She wore a pink tulle skirt and carried a pink parasol in her hand. With delicate little steps she ran out on the rope. She swung her legs gracefully in the air and did all sorts of tricks. It looked so pretty. She even showed how she could walk backward on the narrow rope. But when she got back to the little platform at the end of the rope, there stood Pippi.

"What are you going to do now?" asked Pippi, delighted when she saw how astonished Miss Elvira looked.

Miss Elvira said nothing at all but jumped down from the rope and threw her arms around the ringmaster's neck, for he was her father. And the ringmaster once more sent for his guards to throw Pippi out. This time he sent for five of them, but all the people shouted, "Let her stay! We want to see the red-headed girl." And they stamped their feet and clapped their hands.

Pippi ran out on the rope, and Miss Elvira's tricks were as nothing compared with Pippi's. When she got to the middle of the rope she stretched one leg straight up in the air, and her big shoe spread out like a roof over her head. She bent her foot a little so that she could tickle herself with it back of her ear.

The ringmaster was not at all pleased to have Pippi performing in his circus. He wanted to get rid of her, and so he stole up and loosened the mechanism that held the rope taut, thinking surely Pippi would fall down.

But Pippi didn't. She set the rope a-swinging instead.

Back and forth it swayed, and Pippi swung faster and faster, until suddenly she leaped out into the air and landed right on the ringmaster. He was so frightened he began to run.

"Oh, what a jolly horse!" cried Pippi. "But why don't you have any pompoms in your hair?"

Now Pippi decided it was time to go back to Tommy and Annika. She jumped off the ringmaster and went back to her seat. The next act was about to begin, but there was a brief pause because the ringmaster had to go out and get a drink of water and comb his hair.

Then he came in again, bowed to the audience, and said, "Ladies and gentlemen, in a moment you will be privileged to see the Greatest Marvel of all time, the Strongest Man in the World, the Mighty Adolf, whom no one has yet been able to conquer. Here he comes, ladies and gentlemen. Allow me to present to you THE MIGHTY ADOLF."

And into the ring stepped a man who looked as big as a giant. He wore flesh-colored tights and had a leopard skin draped around his stomach. He bowed to the audience and looked very pleased with himself.

"Look at these muscles," said the ringmaster and squeezed the Mighty Adolf's arm where the muscles stood out like balls under the skin.

"And now, ladies and gentlemen, I have a very special invitation for you. Who will challenge the Mighty Adolf in a wrestling match? Which of you dares to try his strength against the World's Strongest Man? A hundred dollars for anyone who can conquer the Mighty Adolf! A hundred dollars, ladies and gentlemen! Think of that! Who will be the first to try?"

Nobody came forth.

"What did he say?" asked Pippi.

"He says that anybody who can lick that big man will get a hundred dollars," answered Tommy.

"I can," said Pippi, "but I think it would be too bad to, because he looks nice."

"Oh, no, you couldn't," said Annika, "he's the strongest man in the world."

"*Man*, yes," said Pippi, "but I am the strongest *girl* in the world, remember that."

Meanwhile the Mighty Adolf was lifting heavy iron weights and bending thick iron rods in the middle just to show how strong he was.

"Oh, come now, ladies and gentlemen," cried the ringmaster, "is there really nobody here who wants to earn a hundred dollars? Shall I really be forced to keep this myself?" And he waved a bill in the air.

"No, that you certainly won't be forced to do," said Pippi and stepped over the railing into the ring.

The ringmaster was absolutely wild when he saw her. "Get out of here! I don't want to see any more of you," he hissed.

"Why do you always have to be so unfriendly?" said Pippi reproachfully. "I just want to fight with Mighty Adolf."

"This is no place for jokes," said the ringmaster. "Get out of here before the Mighty Adolf hears your impudent nonsense."

But Pippi went right by the ringleader and up to Mighty Adolf. She took his hand and shook it heartily.

"Shall we fight a little, you and I?" she asked.

Mighty Adolf looked at her but didn't understand a word.

"In one minute I'll begin," said Pippi.

And begin she did. She grabbed Mighty Adolf around the waist, and before anyone knew what was happening she had thrown him on the mat. Mighty Adolf leaped up, his face absolutely scarlet.

"Atta girl, Pippi!" shrieked Tommy and Annika, so loudly that all the people at the circus heard it and began to shriek,

"Atta girl, Pippi!" too. The ringmaster sat on the railing, wringing his hands. He was mad, but Mighty Adolf was madder. Never in his life had he experienced anything so humiliating as this. And he certainly intended to show that red-headed girl what kind of a man Mighty Adolf really was. He rushed at Pippi and caught her round the waist, but Pippi stood firm as a rock.

"You can do better than that," she said to encourage him. Then she wriggled out of his grasp, and in the twinkling of an eye Mighty Adolf was on the mat again. Pippi stood beside him, waiting. She didn't have to wait long. With a roar he was up again, rushing at her.

"Tiddelipom and piddeliday," said Pippi.

All the people in the tent stamped their feet and threw their hats in the air and shouted, "Hurrah, Pippi!"

When Mighty Adolf came rushing at her for the third time, Pippi lifted him high in the air and, with her arms straight above her, carried him clear around the ring. Then she laid him down on the mat again and held him there.

"Now, little fellow," said she, "I don't think we'll bother about this any more. We'll never have any more fun than we've had already."

"Pippi is the winner! Pippi is the winner!" cried all the people.

Mighty Adolf stole out as fast as he could, and the ringmaster had to go up and hand Pippi the hundred dollars, although he looked as if he'd much prefer to eat her.

"Here you are, young lady, here you are," he said. "One hundred dollars."

"That thing!" said Pippi scornfully. "What would I want with that old piece of paper. Take it and use it to fry herring on if you want to." And she went back to her seat.

"This is certainly a long surkus," she said to Tommy and

Annika. "I think I'll take a little snooze, but wake me if they need my help with anything else."

And then she lay back in her chair and went to sleep at once. There she lay and snored while the clowns, the sword swallowers, and the snake charmers did their tricks for Tommy and Annika and all the rest of the people at the circus.

"Just the same, I think Pippi was best of all," whispered Tommy to Annika.

# Encyclopedia Brown

from *Encyclopedia Brown and the Case of the Secret Pitch*
by Donald J. Sobol
illustrated by Leonard Shortall
**LODESTAR BOOKS, 1965**

# About Encyclopedia Brown

No case is too small to receive the attention of Encyclopedia Brown, America's favorite sleuth in sneakers. Encyclopedia runs his own detective agency in the Brown garage, and his fee is only twenty-five cents a day plus expenses. Whether he is unraveling a mysterious kidnapping or outwitting a cowardly bully, the ten-year-old detective always finds the solution. Readers have a chance to match wits with Encyclopedia by following the logical clues before consulting the answers included with each mystery.

"Readers constantly ask me if Encyclopedia Brown is a real boy," Donald J. Sobol says. "The answer is no. He is, perhaps, the boy I wanted to be—doing the things I wanted to read about but could not find in any book when I was ten." Ever since the first Encyclopedia Brown mystery was published in 1963, millions of young readers have become fans of the popular boy detective. *The Case of the Secret Pitch*, published in 1965, is the second title in the series, which has now reached twenty books. In addition, Encyclopedia Brown books include the Wacky series, a cookbook, the *Book of Strange But True Crimes* (with Rose Sobol, his wife), and several Encyclopedia Brown Record Books of Weird and Wonderful Facts.

**Donald J. Sobol** grew up in New York City and has made Florida his home for many years. He worked as a copyboy, a journalist, and a retailer before turning to writing full-time. His first best-seller was *Two Flags Flying*, which *The New York Times* listed as one of the ten all-time best books for young readers about the Civil War. He has written more than sixty-five books, and his books have been translated into fifteen languages, including Chinese. He has also written an international syndicated newspaper feature, "Two Minute Mystery Series," and hundreds of stories and articles for adult magazines. He prefers writing for young people.

# The Case of the Secret Pitch

Idaville looked like any other town of its size—from the outside.

On the inside, however, it was different. Ten-year-old Encyclopedia Brown, America's Sherlock Holmes in sneakers, lived there.

Besides Encyclopedia, Idaville had three movie theaters, a Little League, four banks, and two delicatessens. It had large houses and small houses, good schools, churches, stores, and even an ugly old section by the railroad tracks.

And it had, everyone believed, the best police force in the world.

For more than a year no one—boy, girl, or grown-up—had got away with breaking a single law.

Encyclopedia's father was chief of police. People said he was the smartest chief of police in the world and his officers were the best trained and the bravest. Chief Brown knew better.

His men were brave, true enough. They did their jobs well. But Chief Brown brought his hardest cases home for Encyclopedia to solve.

For a year now Chief Brown had been getting the answers during dinner in his red brick house on Rover Avenue. He never told a soul. How could he?

Who would believe that the guiding hand behind Idaville's crime cleanup wore a junior-size baseball mitt?

Encyclopedia never let out the secret, either. He didn't want to seem different from other fifth-graders.

There was nothing he could do about his nickname, however.

An encyclopedia is a book or set of books filled with facts on all subjects. Encyclopedia had read so many books his head held more facts than a library.

Nobody but his teachers and his parents called him by his real name, Leroy. He was called Encyclopedia by everyone else in Idaville.

Encyclopedia did not do all his crime-busting seated at the dinner table. During the summer he usually solved mysteries while walking around.

Soon after vacation began, he had opened his own detective business. He wanted to help others.

Children seeking help of every kind came to his office in the Brown garage. Encyclopedia handled each case himself. The terms of his business were clearly stated on the sign that hung outside the garage.

One morning Speedy Flanagan, the shortest fast-ball pitcher in the Idaville Little League, walked into the Brown Detective Agency. He wore a face longer than the last day of school.

"I need help," he said, side-arming twenty-five cents into the gasoline can beside Encyclopedia. "What do you know about Browning?"

"Nothing, I've never browned," replied Encyclopedia. "But once at the beach I tanned something awful, and—"

"I mean Robert Browning," said Speedy.

"The English poet?"

"No, no," said Speedy. "The American League pitcher, Robert *Spike* Browning."

Even Encyclopedia's Aunt Bessie knew of Spike Browning. He was the ace of the New York Yankees' pitching staff.

"What do you want to know about him?" asked Encyclopedia.

"Do you know what his handwriting looks like?" asked Speedy. "I made a bet with Bugs Meany—my bat against his—that Bugs couldn't get Spike Browning to buy a secret pitch for a hundred dollars."

"Whoa!" cried Encyclopedia. "If I understand you, Bugs bet he could sell Spike Browning a special way to throw a base-ball?"

"Right. Bugs and his father were in New York City the last week in June," said Speedy. "Bugs says he sold Spike Browning his cross-eyed special."

"You'd better explain," said Encyclopedia.

"The pitcher crosses his eyes whenever there are runners on first and third bases," said Speedy. "That way nobody knows where he's looking—whether he's going to throw to first base, third base, or home plate. The runners don't dare take a lead. The secret is how the pitcher can throw the ball some place while staring himself in the eye. Bugs sold the secret. He has a letter from Spike Browning and a check for a hundred dollars!"

"Phew!" said Encyclopedia. "I understand you now. You figure Bugs wrote the letter and the check himself to win the bet and your bat. So do I! Let's go see Bugs."

Bugs Meany was the leader of the Tigers, a gang of older boys who caused more trouble than itching powder in Friday's wash. Since setting up as a detective, Encyclopedia had stopped many of Bugs' shady deals.

The Tigers' clubhouse was a tool shed behind Mr. Sweeny's Auto Body Shop. When Encyclopedia and Speedy arrived, Bugs was leading a discussion on how to beat the bubble gum machines around town.

The Tigers' leader broke off to greet Encyclopedia. "Get lost," he said.

"Not until I have a chance to see the letter and check from Spike Browning," said Encyclopedia.

Bugs opened a cigar box and passed Encyclopedia a check and a letter. Encyclopedia read the letter.

Yankee Stadium, New York
June 31

Dear Bugs:

Your cross-eyed pitch is the greatest
thing since the spitball. I expect to win thirty
games with it this season.

For sole rights to the secret of it, I'm happy
to enclose my check for one hundred dollars.

Yours truly,

Spike Browning

The letter was written on plain white paper. The check, bearing the same date as the letter, was drawn on the First National Bank for one hundred dollars.

"Spike will win fifty games this season," said Bugs. "And I won one baseball bat from Speedy Flanagan. So where is it?"

"Where's *your* bat?" corrected Encyclopedia. "Speedy won the bet. You lost. The letter and check are fakes."

"I ought to shove those words down your throat," said Bugs. "But I'm feeling too good about what I did for the great American game of baseball."

Bugs crossed his eyes. Humming to himself, he went into his secret throwing motion. The other Tigers cheered wildly.

"Man, oh man!" sang Bugs. "I invented the greatest pitch since Edison threw out the gas lamp. No smart-aleck private detective is going to walk in here and call me a liar!"

"Oh, yes I am," said Encyclopedia. "Spike Browning never wrote that letter. That check is a worthless piece of paper!"

## WHAT MADE ENCYCLOPEDIA SO CERTAIN?
### Solution to *The Case of the Secret Pitch*

Encyclopedia knew instantly that neither the letter nor the check was written by the Yankee pitcher, Spike Browning, nor by any grown-up.

Both the check and the letter bore the same date—June 31, but no year was given.

*And there is no June 31.* June has only 30 days!

Shown the errors, Bugs could do nothing but admit having written the letter and check himself. As the loser of the bet, he had to give Speedy Flanagan his baseball bat.

# Matilda

from *Matilda* by Roald Dahl,
illustrated by Quentin Blake
THE VIKING PRESS, 1988

# About Matilda

*Matilda,* said Roald Dahl, is "different from the others. This one has a good crack at illiterate parents and also at insensitive teachers. It is also a song of praise for good teachers and for reading books." Matilda, a brilliant child, takes to reading the classics at a very young age. Of his own reading history, Dahl said, "Because of the shortage of children's books . . . we very rapidly graduated to more adult fiction. . . . At the age of fourteen, I think I had read just about every great classic in literature, as well as plenty of others. . . . We loved books. We were brought up on them."

**Roald Dahl,** 1916–1990, was born in Wales, the son of Norwegian immigrants. His writing career began with one short story published in *The Saturday Evening Post.* It wasn't until he had established himself as a successful writer of adult fiction that Dahl moved on to writing for children. He wrote more than twenty books for children. Three of his novels, *James and the Giant Peach, Charlie and the Chocolate Factory,* and *Matilda,* were instant classics and have all been made into popular films.

**Quentin Blake** began illustrating professionally while still in his teens. He has written and/or illustrated over two hundred books for children.

Matilda was a little late in starting school. Most children begin Primary School at five or even just before, but Matilda's parents, who weren't very concerned one way or the other about their daughter's education, had forgotten to make the proper arrangements in advance. She was five and a half when she entered school for the first time.

The village school for younger children was a bleak brick building called Crunchem Hall Primary School. It had about two hundred and fifty pupils aged from five to just under twelve years old. The head teacher, the boss, the supreme commander of this establishment was a formidable middle-aged lady whose name was Miss Trunchbull.

Naturally Matilda was put in the bottom class, where there were eighteen other small boys and girls about the same age as her. Their teacher was called Miss Honey, and she could not have been more than twenty-three or twenty-four. She had a lovely pale oval madonna face with blue eyes and her hair was light-brown. Her body was so slim and fragile one got the feeling that if she fell over she would smash into a thousand pieces, like a porcelain figure.

Miss Jennifer Honey was a mild and quiet person who never raised her voice and was seldom seen to smile, but there is no doubt she possessed that rare gift for being adored by every small child under her care. She seemed to understand totally the bewilderment and fear that so often overwhelms young children who for the first time in their lives are herded into a classroom and told to obey orders. Some curious warmth that was almost tangible shone out of Miss Honey's face when she spoke to a confused and homesick newcomer to the class.

Miss Trunchbull, the Headmistress, was something else altogether. She was a gigantic holy terror, a fierce tyrannical monster who frightened the life out of the pupils and teachers alike. There was an aura of menace about her even at a distance, and when she came up close you could almost feel the dangerous heat radiating from her as from a red-hot rod of metal. When she marched—Miss Trunchbull never walked, she always marched like a stormtrooper with long strides and arms aswinging—when she marched along a corridor you could actually hear her snorting as she went, and if a group of children happened to be in her path, she ploughed right on through them like a tank, with small people bouncing off her to left and right. Thank goodness we don't meet many people like her in this world, although they do exist and all of us are likely to come across at least one of them in a lifetime. If you ever do, you should behave as you would if you met an enraged rhinoceros out in the bush—climb up the nearest tree and stay there until it has gone away. This woman, in all her eccentricities and in her appearance, is almost impossible to describe, but I shall make some attempt to do so a little later on. Let us leave her for the moment and go back to Matilda and her first day in Miss Honey's class.

After the usual business of going through all the names of the children, Miss Honey handed out a brand-new exercise-book to each pupil.

"You have all brought your own pencils, I hope," she said.

"Yes, Miss Honey," they chanted.

"Good. Now this is the very first day of school for each one of you. It is the beginning of at least eleven long years of schooling that all of you are going to have to go through. And six of those years will be spent right here at Crunchem Hall where, as you know, your Headmistress is Miss Trunchbull. Let me for your own good tell you something about Miss Trunchbull. She insists upon strict discipline throughout the school, and if you take my advice you will do your very best to behave yourselves in her presence. Never argue with her. Never answer her back. Always do as she says. If you get on the wrong side of Miss Trunchbull she can liquidise you like a carrot in a kitchen blender. It's nothing to laugh about, Lavender. Take that grin off your face. All of you will be wise to remember that Miss Trunchbull deals very very severely with anyone who gets out of line in this school. Have you got the message?"

"Yes, Miss Honey," chirruped eighteen eager little voices.

"I myself," Miss Honey went on, "want to help you to learn as much as possible while you are in this class. That is because I know it will make things easier for you later on. For example, by the end of this week I shall expect every one of you to know the two-times table by heart. And in a year's time I hope you will know all the multiplication tables up to twelve. It will help you enormously if you do. Now then, do any of you happen to have learnt the two-times table already?"

Matilda put up her hand. She was the only one.

Miss Honey looked carefully at the tiny girl with dark hair and a round serious face sitting in the second row. "Wonderful," she said. "Please stand up and recite as much of it as you can."

Matilda stood up and began to say the two-times table. When she got to twice twelve is twenty-four she didn't stop. She went right on with twice thirteen is twenty-six, twice fourteen is twenty-eight, twice fifteen is thirty, twice sixteen is . . ."

"Stop!" Miss Honey said. She had been listening slightly spellbound to this smooth recital, and now she said, "How far can you go?"

"How far?" Matilda said. "Well, I don't really know, Miss Honey. For quite a long way, I think."

Miss Honey took a few moments to let this curious statement sink in. "You mean," she said, "that you could tell me what two times twenty-eight is?"

"Yes, Miss Honey."

"What is it?"

"Fifty-six, Miss Honey."

"What about something much harder, like two times four hundred and eighty-seven? Could you tell me that?"

"I think so, yes," Matilda said.

"Are you sure?"

"Why yes, Miss Honey, I'm fairly sure."

"What is it then, two times four hundred and eighty-seven?"

"Nine hundred and seventy-four," Matilda said immediately. She spoke quietly and politely and without any sign of showing off.

Miss Honey gazed at Matilda with absolute amazement, but when next she spoke she kept her voice level. "That is really splendid," she said. "But of course multiplying by two is a lot easier than some of the bigger numbers. What about the other multiplication tables? Do you know any of those?"

"I think so, Miss Honey. I think I do."

"Which ones, Matilda? How far have you got?"

"I . . . I don't quite know," Matilda said. "I don't know what you mean."

"What I mean is do you for instance know the three-times table?"

"Yes, Miss Honey."

"And the four-times?"

"Yes, Miss Honey."

"Well, how many *do* you know, Matilda? Do you know all the way up to the twelve-times table?"

"Yes, Miss Honey."

"What are twelve sevens?"

"Eighty-four," Matilda said.

Miss Honey paused and leaned back in her chair behind the plain table that stood in the middle of the floor in front of the class. She was considerably shaken by this exchange but took care not to show it. She had never come across a five-year-old before, or indeed a ten-year-old, who could multiply with such facility.

"I hope the rest of you are listening to this," she said to the class. "Matilda is a very lucky girl. She has wonderful parents who have already taught her to multiply lots of numbers. Was it your mother, Matilda, who taught you?"

"No, Miss Honey, it wasn't."

"You must have a great father then. He must be a brilliant teacher."

"No, Miss Honey," Matilda said quietly. "My father did not teach me."

"You mean you taught yourself?"

"I don't quite know," Matilda said truthfully. "It's just that I don't find it very difficult to multiply one number by another."

Miss Honey took a deep breath and let it out slowly. She looked again at the small girl with bright eyes standing beside her desk so sensible and solemn. "You say you don't find it difficult to multiply one number by another," Miss Honey said. "Could you try to explain that a little bit."

"Oh dear," Matilda said. "I'm not really sure."

Miss Honey waited. The class was silent, all listening.

"For instance," Miss Honey said, "if I asked you to multiply fourteen by nineteen . . . No, that's too difficult . . ."

"It's two hundred and sixty-six," Matilda said softly.

Miss Honey stared at her. Then she picked up a pencil and quickly worked out the sum on a piece of paper. "What did you say it was?" she said, looking up.

"Two hundred and sixty-six," Matilda said.

Miss Honey put down her pencil and removed her spectacles and began to polish the lenses with a piece of tissue. The class remained quiet, watching her and waiting for what was

coming next. Matilda was still standing up beside her desk.

"Now tell me, Matilda," Miss Honey said, still polishing, "try to tell me exactly what goes on inside your head when you get a multiplication like that to do. You obviously have to work it out in some way, but you seem able to arrive at the answer almost instantly. Take the one you've just done, fourteen multiplied by nineteen."

"I . . . I . . . I simply put the fourteen down in my head and multiply it by nineteen," Matilda said. "I'm afraid I don't know how else to explain it. I've always said to myself that if a little pocket calculator can do it why shouldn't I?"

"Why not indeed," Miss Honey said. "The human brain is an amazing thing."

"I think it's a lot better than a lump of metal," Matilda said. "That's all a calculator is."

"How right you are," Miss Honey said. "Pocket calculators are not allowed in this school anyway." Miss Honey was feeling quite quivery. There was no doubt in her mind that she had met a truly extraordinary mathematical brain, and words like child-genius and prodigy went flitting through her head. She knew that these sort of wonders do pop up in the world from time to time, but only once or twice in a hundred years. After all, Mozart was only five when he started composing for the piano and look what happened to him.

"It's not fair," Lavender said. "How can she do it and we can't?"

"Don't worry, Lavender, you'll soon catch up," Miss Honey said, lying through her teeth.

At this point Miss Honey could not resist the temptation of exploring still further the mind of this astonishing child. She knew that she ought to be paying some attention to the rest of the class but she was altogether too excited to let the matter rest.

"Well," she said, pretending to address the whole class, "let us leave sums for the moment and see if any of you have begun to learn to spell. Hands up anyone who can spell cat."

Three hands went up. They belonged to Lavender, a small boy called Nigel and to Matilda.

"Spell cat, Nigel."

Nigel spelled it.

Miss Honey now decided to ask a question that normally she would not have dreamed of asking the class on its first day. "I wonder," she said, "whether any of you three who know how to spell cat have learned how to read a whole group of words when they are strung together in a sentence?"

"I have," Nigel said.

"So have I," Lavender said.

Miss Honey went to the blackboard and wrote with her white chalk the sentence, *I have already begun to learn how to read long sentences.* She had purposely made it difficult and she knew that there were precious few five-year-olds around who would be able to manage it.

"Can you tell me what that says, Nigel?" she asked.

"That's too hard," Nigel said.

"Lavender?"

"The first word is I," Lavender said.

"Can any of you read the whole sentence?" Miss Honey asked, waiting for the "yes" that she felt certain was going to come from Matilda.

"Yes," Matilda said.

"Go ahead," Miss Honey said.

Matilda read the sentence without any hesitation at all.

"That really is very good indeed," Miss Honey said, making the understatement of her life. "How much *can* you read, Matilda?"

"I think I can read most things, Miss Honey," Matilda said, "although I'm afraid I can't always understand the meanings."

Miss Honey got to her feet and walked smartly out of the room, but was back in thirty seconds carrying a thick book. She opened it at random and placed it on Matilda's desk. "This is a book of humorous poetry," she said. "See if you can read that one aloud."

Smoothly, without a pause and at a nice speed, Matilda began to read:

"An epicure dining at Crewe
Found a rather large mouse in his stew.

Cried the waiter, "Don't shout
And wave it about
Or the rest will be wanting one too."

Several children saw the funny side of the rhyme and laughed. Miss Honey said, "Do you know what an epicure is, Matilda?"

"It is someone who is dainty with his eating," Matilda said.

"That is correct," Miss Honey said. "And do you happen to know what that particular type of poetry is called?"

"It's called a limerick," Matilda said. "That's a lovely one. It's so funny."

"It's a famous one," Miss Honey said, picking up the book and returning to her table in front of the class. "A witty limerick is very hard to write," she added. "They look easy but they most certainly are not."

"I know," Matilda said. "I've tried quite a few times but mine are never any good."

"You have, have you?" Miss Honey said, more startled than ever. "Well Matilda, I would very much like to hear one of these limericks you say you have written. Could you try to remember one for us?"

"Well," Matilda said, hesitating. "I've actually been trying to make up one about you, Miss Honey, while we've been sitting here."

"About *me*!" Miss Honey cried. "Well, we've certainly got to hear that one, haven't we?"

"I don't think I want to say it, Miss Honey."

"Please tell it," Miss Honey said. "I promise I won't mind."

"I think you will, Miss Honey, because I have to use your first name to make things rhyme and that's why I don't want to say it."

"How do you know my first name?" Miss Honey asked.

"I heard another teacher calling you by it just before we came in," Matilda said. "She called you Jenny."

"I insist upon hearing this limerick," Miss Honey said, smiling one of her rare smiles. "Stand up and recite it."

Reluctantly Matilda stood up and very slowly, very nervously, she recited her limerick:

"The thing we all ask about Jenny
Is, 'Surely there cannot be many
Young girls in the place
With so lovely a face?'
The answer to that is, *'Not any!'*"

The whole of Miss Honey's pale and pleasant face blushed a brilliant scarlet. Then once again she smiled. It was a much broader one this time, a smile of pure pleasure.

"Why, thank you, Matilda," she said, still smiling. "Although it is not true, it is really a very good limerick. Oh dear, oh dear, I must try to remember that one."

From the third row of desks, Lavender said, "It's good. I like it."

"It's true as well," a small boy called Rupert said.

"Of course it's true," Nigel said.

Already the whole class had begun to warm towards Miss Honey, although as yet she had hardly taken any notice of any of them except Matilda.

"Who taught you to read, Matilda?" Miss Honey asked.

"I just sort of taught myself, Miss Honey."

"And have you read any books all by yourself, any children's books, I mean?"

"I've read all the ones that are in the public library in the High Street, Miss Honey."

"And did you like them?"

"I liked some of them very much indeed," Matilda said, "but I thought others were fairly dull."

"Tell me one that you liked."

"I liked *The Lion, the Witch and the Wardrobe*," Matilda said. "I think Mr C. S. Lewis is a very good writer. But he has one failing. There are no funny bits in his books."

"You are right there," Miss Honey said.

"There aren't many funny bits in Mr Tolkien either," Matilda said.

"Do you think that all children's books ought to have funny bits in them?" Miss Honey asked.

"I do," Matilda said. "Children are not so serious as grown-ups and they love to laugh."

Miss Honey was astounded by the wisdom of this tiny girl. She said, "And what are you going to do now that you've read all the children's books?"

"I am reading other books," Matilda said. "I borrow them from the library. Mrs Phelps is very kind to me. She helps me to choose them."

Miss Honey was leaning far forward over her work-table and gazing in wonder at the child. She had completely forgotten now about the rest of the class. "What other books?" she murmured.

"I am very fond of Charles Dickens," Matilda said. "He makes me laugh a lot. Especially Mr Pickwick."

At that moment the bell in the corridor sounded for the end of class.

# Sebastian

from *The Marvelous Misadventures of Sebastian*
by Lloyd Alexander
**DUTTON CHILDREN'S BOOKS, 1970**

# About Sebastian

When *The Marvelous Misadventures of Sebastian* won the 1971 National Book Award, author Lloyd Alexander thanked his listeners with a characteristically modest reference to himself as "the worst fiddler of all times." An avid lover of Mozart, Alexander took up the violin as an adult, and it continues to be one of his primary interests. For that reason, fans who know him best find a special delight in following the thrilling and circuitous fortunes of Sebastian, a court musician, who loses his post of Fourth Fiddler and sets off as a beggar, only to discover an indomitable princess in disguise, a wise feline traveling companion, and transforming truths in the strangest places. As the author has said, "The story isn't only about a musician. Fantasy should speak from and to the human condition, and I think each of us carries Sebastian's fiddle in one form or another. The question is: How closely dare we listen to it? How deeply are we willing to commit ourselves to its music? Sebastian heard his own answer, as we must hear our own melodies."

Born in 1924, **Lloyd Alexander** decided he wanted to be a writer at the age of fifteen. He had no idea how to begin, but later remarked that "If reading offered preparation for writing, there were grounds for hope." Wending his way through early adulthood and careers as a bank messenger, World War II intelligence officer and artilleryman, cymbal player, cartoonist, and magazine editor, he produced manuscript after manuscript until his first book was accepted for publication. But in 1963, he turned his attention to writing for children, and *Time Cat* became the first in a series of novels that would reshape the landscape of children's fantasy forever. Winner of the Newbery Medal for *The High King* and a Newbery Honor for *The Black Cauldron*— two of the five volumes in the Chronicles of Prydain—and recipient of the Regina Medal, Lloyd Alexander lives with his wife, Janine, in Drexel Hill, Pennsylvania.

# How Sebastian Found a Friend

The prospect of being thrown into jail, on top of all his other griefs, shook Sebastian from his daze. Clutching his bag under one arm and mopping his bleeding nose with his jacket sleeve, he set off as fast as his legs would carry him. He left the road at the first open field he came to, and cut across it until he could not be seen easily, fearful the witch-trappers might still be seeking their victim.

"And from what I've seen of Skimmerhorn and Spargel," he told himself, "they'd be just as happy to have me in their net."

At last, too weary to go farther, he sat down by a thicket near a stream and drew out the shattered fiddle to examine it more closely, hoping the damage was not quite as bad as it first had seemed. But the fiddle was indeed beyond repair. Sebastian shook his head.

"Well, there goes Spire—and Darmstel, New Locking, and Loringhold," he sighed, tossing the useless instrument into the bushes.

He turned away, then looked back in surprise. A pair of blue eyes was watching him from the thicket.

In another moment, the white cat picked its way out of the underbrush and padded toward him.

"Aha, so it's you," Sebastian said, brightening a little. He held out his hands to the cat, who circled him slowly for a careful look at its rescuer. "Between the two of us, I think you've fared better than I. For I've lost my place, lost my living, lost my supper, and had my nose punched into the bargain, all in the same day."

The white cat began sniffing Sebastian's fingers.

"Alas, I've nothing for you," Sebastian said. "Unless you're truly a witch, and conjure me up a roasted chicken and a new fiddle, I've nothing for myself either. I'll tell you truthfully, as things have gone with me, you'll do better to make your own way."

The cat, instead of taking Sebastian's advice, sat on its haunches and watched him boldly.

"Well, at least I'll do what I can for that ear of yours," Sebastian told him. "Come along, then."

Without warning, the cat suddenly tensed its muscles and leaped straight to Sebastian's shoulder, nearly knocking him off balance with the force of the spring.

"How now, are you cat or monkey?" Sebastian cried. "Let me know when you mean to play that trick again."

At the stream, he tore a bit of cloth from his shirt, dipped it in the water, and dabbed as gently as he could at the cat's injured ear. But after a moment, the cat struggled and twisted away to jump to the ground.

The animal moistened a forepaw with its tongue and painstakingly began scrubbing from the tips of its ears to the ends of its whiskers; then turned its attention to its muddy fur, licking it vigorously, ducking its head in every direction so as not to overlook any part of itself; and all in all doing a more workmanlike job than Sebastian could have accomplished.

"Well, you're a handsome fellow, and make a better showing now than you did when first we met," Sebastian said, rubbing a finger under the cat's jaws. Bigger than it had seemed in the net, the cat's body was long, lean, sleek as an otter, and pure white from head to tail. Neck and shoulders were smoothly but powerfully muscled, the tips of the curving claws glittered like dagger points, and the cat's whole bearing was that of a wild creature more used to forests than to firesides.

Stroking the cat's head, Sebastian stopped when he touched the ridge of a heavy scar at the side of the animal's throat. "I can see you've been in more than one battle," he said, finding another long-healed wound under the fur of the cat's chest. "If you could talk, as those cowards in Dorn believed, you could surely tell me a few tales. Very well, if you mean to stay, make yourself comfortable. Though I doubt if I'll be able to do the same."

Sebastian gave his new friend a final pat and looked unhappily at the bushes that would have to serve as a bed.

Dusk was gathering quickly. Trampling the turf as smooth as he could, and longing for the Merry Host's bale of hay, Sebastian curled up awkwardly, with his green bag tucked under his head for a pillow.

He shut his eyes, hoping a night's sleep would be his best remedy. Instead, as he settled himself, the weight of the past day suddenly toppled on him. His nose throbbed, his head ached; and despite his brave words and bright hopes, with all his heart he wished himself back in the musicians' quarters, his hunger satisfied, his fiddle unbroken. Like a child, he tried to pretend that no disaster had really happened; that when he opened his eyes again, all would be as it had always been, with the First Fiddle shaking him out of bed; that The Purse, the Merry Host, Skimmerhorn, and Spargel were no more than a bad dream. Then he pressed his face into the makeshift pillow and wept as he had never done in all his life.

There was a faint rustling, and he started up. The cat had come to curl beside him, purring softly. Sebastian sank back and drew closer to the warmth of the furry body. In a while, he slept, holding the cat in his arms as if it were his last and only comfort; as indeed it was.

When he woke in the morning, his clothes were sopping with dew and he had a crick in his neck. But his spirits were higher than they had been the night before.

"Lost my living? No! My fiddle's ruined, that's true, and I can't buy another. But wherever I find a place, they'll have one I can borrow to prove my skill. And if I play well enough—why, they might make me a gift of any fiddle I want!"

Taking courage from this new thought, he jumped to his feet, waved his arms to shake off the morning chill and unknot his cramped muscles, and felt eager to start on his way again.

The cat had come bounding up from the stream. Sebastian clapped his hands and called out:

"Come along! With luck, I'll find a place for both of us. But hurry! *Hop-la! Presto! Prestissimo!*"

Without breaking stride, the cat leaped straight for Sebastian's shoulder, and clung there, purring happily, flirting its whiskers, and seeming to grin proudly at its own trick.

"Presto?" Sebastian repeated. "You're quick enough to be called that. Whatever your name before, if you had any at all, Presto you are and Presto you'll be."

With the cat draped like a white scarf over one shoulder and his green bag bouncing on the other, Sebastian set off in what he hoped was the direction of Spire. The crick in his neck had gone, but his appetite was roaring like a furnace; before he undertook to find a place, he would first have to find something to eat. The longer he walked, the hungrier he grew. His head pounded like a kettledrum and he felt a little giddy.

"I don't know how long it takes to starve," he said to the cat, "but I think I've well begun."

By this time of morning, he thought ruefully, Baron Purn-Hessel's cook would be handing him a second cup of chocolate and a third piece of cake; but these memories only sharpened his appetite. By the time he reached the outskirts of Spire, he was jogging along as fast as he could, ready to trade future fortune for present breakfast.

In his mind's ear, the name of Spire had rung like a golden bell in a golden steeple. Reaching the middle of the town, he found it not gold but gray. Though he had taken the precaution of carrying Presto in the green bag, for the cat's own safety as well as to avoid idle curiosity, he soon realized that he could have walked the narrow, muddy streets with Presto perched on top of his head, for all the folk of Spire would have noticed. Housewives with market baskets, soldiers with pistols in their belts and sabers rattling at their sides, tradesmen, and shabbily dressed children jostled along with never a glance at him. The faces of the passersby seemed pinched and tightly drawn. They kept their eyes straight ahead, looking neither left nor right, and hurried anxiously on their way.

To Sebastian's disappointment, the opera house and theatre had been closed and turned into barracks for a new garrison of the Regent's dragoons. He learned this from the first passerby he ventured to ask: a carpenter who seemed frightened out of his wits at being stopped and questioned, who stammered out the information most unwillingly and set off again with all speed.

Sebastian shook his head. The air of Spire had begun to weigh on him and make him as uneasy as the rest of the towns- folk. "Did I ever hope to find a place here?" he muttered to Presto, who peered up at him from the depths of the bag. "Why, it seems worth a man's neck to give you the time of day! And that poor devil of a carpenter—you might have thought I was the Regent himself, he was so glad to be shut of me! Well, no matter. Darmstel's bound to have better cheer. In any case, it surely can't be worse."

Before pressing on, however, Sebastian realized he would have to answer his appetite or collapse on the spot. His eyes brightened at the sight of a bakeshop and he stepped inside, joining the crowd of errand boys, housewives, and servant girls elbowing each other for places at the counter.

The flour-daubed baker and his apprentice shoveled hot loaves from the oven; the baker-woman, as stout as if she had risen with her own yeast, was selling her wares so quickly that Sebastian feared none would be left when it came his turn. He waited impatiently, drinking in the aroma, delighting himself by trying to decide between a long, a round, or a square loaf, tast- ing each in his imagination.

Finally at the counter, he was too hungry to care about shape and simply pointed eagerly at the biggest loaf he saw, crisp and golden-crusted, looking half the size of a millstone. His face fell, however, when he reached into his pocket. His fingers found only a ragged hole, torn, most likely, during the scuffle at the Merry Host. His coins were gone.

"My money—I can't find it," he stammered as the baker-woman held out her hand. Hastily, he pulled all his pockets inside out, hoping the coins were only misplaced. The search yielded nothing.

The baker-woman snatched back the loaf as if it were the crown jewels of Hamelin-Loring. "Go play your jokes elsewhere," she cried, "and let honest folk be served."

The crowd behind him grumbled, jostled, and called for him to step aside. Sebastian, roughly shoved from the counter, turned to the baker.

"My money's lost, but I'll pay with my work," he offered. "Let me clean your oven, or sweep—"

The baker looked at him suspiciously. "What's your trade?"

"I'm a fiddler," Sebastian began. "But—"

"Then go fiddle!" returned the baker. "I say: a place for every man and every man in his place. And why you're out of yours is no business of mine."

So saying, the baker went back to plying his long-handled wooden shovel, pulling loaf after loaf out of the oven.

Baffled, Sebastian lingered at the fringe of the crowd. The smell of bread made his head spin and his mouth water. He breathed deeply, trying to feed on the delicious odor, but this made him only hungrier. Near the counter, a trestle table held a large mixing bowl, a basin of flour, and a pot of butter. Amid these he glimpsed a basket of eggs that drew him like a lodestone. He edged his way to the table.

For long moments he gazed wistfully at the smooth, shining eggs, which now appeared the most beautiful objects he had ever seen. He tasted them soft-boiled, hard-boiled, fried, poached, beaten into an omelette, or even raw. He set his teeth, trying to pull himself away. While serving Baron Purn-Hessel, he would never have hesitated a moment to make free of any dainties lying on the Chief Cook's table; in fact, he often suspected the cook left them there on purpose to be snatched away. But Spire, as he was all too well aware, was not the Baron's estate. The eggs were the baker's, not the Chief Cook's.

Sebastian's fingers twitched, his hands trembled in fear. Try as he would, he could not turn his eyes from the eggs, which grew bigger, brighter, and tastier the longer he stared at them. At last, his hunger overcame his conscience. He could struggle no more. Glancing over his shoulder, he stepped closer to the table, seized three of the eggs, and slipped them into his shirt.

He could not resist a fourth. As he picked it up, the baker's boy spied him and cried:

"Stop, thief!"

# How Sebastian Had a Bucket on His Head

The idea so fired Sebastian's imagination that he saw himself already mounted on a high-spirited stallion galloping across the countryside. Ready to set off instantly, he clapped Nicholas on the back and cried:

"Did I say a fiddler could do nothing against the Regent? Here's my chance! I'd sooner ride with the Captain than scrape away in some noble idiot's orchestra! And you, my friend, come along! We'll find the Captain and both join him!"

But Nicholas, instead of eagerly agreeing, only looked uncomfortable. "The Captain—ah, well, now, there's no doubt he's a bold fellow to challenge the Regent. As for joining him, that's a different matter. It's not a quiet life, with a price on your head and the Regent's dragoons on your heels."

While saying this, he took Sebastian's arm and began gently but firmly leading him along the highway again, at a faster pace than before. Sebastian fell silent, disappointed at his friend's reluctance. Much as he would hate to part from

Nicholas, he nevertheless resolved to seek out the Captain one way or another.

The road menders were soon far behind. But if Nicholas had seemed anxious to reach Darmstel quickly, the closer he came to the town the more unwilling he appeared to enter it.

"You're a strange traveler," Sebastian remarked, puzzled, as Nicholas deliberately turned off the road at the very outskirts of Darmstel and began making his way along hedges and across ditches. "I grant you the Royal Highway's not very royal and not very much of a way, but I like it better than crawling through brambles."

By now, they were approaching the town from an altogether different direction. No sooner did Sebastian glimpse the market square than Nicholas halted and drew back once again. Half-a-dozen dragoons stood by their horses at the watering trough, while a couple more loitered by the shop fronts. Looking closer, Sebastian realized there were still others at the street corners.

"Nicholas, what's amiss?" he murmured uneasily.

"Two hangings, as the road mender told us," Nicholas answered grimly. "But that's far from the end of it. Two lives? Not enough to satisfy Grinssorg. His bloodhounds are surely trying to ferret out the poor devils' friends and families. And anyone else who might side against the Regent."

"And the townsfolk? They'll do nothing?"

"They may try, but the dragoons are there to put down whatever trouble starts. And they'll stop and search every stranger they see in Darmstel. Since I don't relish standing against a wall with a dragoon's bayonet in my ribs and my pockets turned inside out—we'd better wait for a while."

"A shame the Captain isn't here," Sebastian exclaimed. "He'd be more than a match for a whole company of dragoons."

Nicholas shrugged and said no more, and not until dusk was he willing to venture into the town. Though the streets, by now, had fallen into heavy shadow and lights glimmered only here and there, he found his way to the Golden Stag with surprising ease. And so quickly that Sebastian wondered if his strange friend could see as well as Presto in the dark.

Unlike the Merry Host, the proprietor of the Golden Stag appeared open-faced and good-natured; and, as Nicholas had foretold, he was willing to give Sebastian not only lodging for the night but supper, too. While Presto crouched by the fireplace and surveyed the company with as much satisfaction as if he were the host, Sebastian sat down to his meal. Nicholas, meanwhile, had begun some private conversation with the innkeeper. Sebastian could neither overhear nor guess the subject of their talk, but Nicholas frowned in concern and the innkeeper appeared tense and uneasy. Although the eating room was filled, the guests showed no sign of good cheer, but spoke either in low voices or not at all, and their expressions were half-bitter, half-brooding.

This mood of the Golden Stag, instead of raising Sebastian's spirits, only turned his thoughts inward; and he admitted to himself that he truly had no clear idea what to do next. Absorbed in trying to sort out all that had happened to him in so short a time, and to set some plan for the future, he was startled by a voice in his ear:

"Traveled some distance, your honor?"

It was Sebastian's table mate who had spoken: a foppishly dressed man, somewhat less than middle height, with a close-shaven, puffy face pale as a fish belly, and with a jaunty spray of lace for a neckcloth. The stranger wore no wig, but his drab hair was so fancily twirled and teased that Sebastian could hardly tell the difference; and about the fellow hung a cloying scent of pomades, lotions, and aromatic ointments.

"Why, so I have," Sebastian replied, "and I suppose I have still farther to go."

"At your service, then, your worship," said the man, smiling and bending most humbly and fawningly. "Would you be shaved? Your hair powdered? A tooth drawn? Blood let?" His fingers, very fleshy and flexible, meantime were deftly undoing the buckles of a black leather case, which opened to reveal not only bottles of perfume and cakes of soap, but also an assortment of lancets, razors, a jar of squirming leeches, and a number of glittering, cruel-looking surgical instruments.

"Spare your pains and mine," Sebastian answered, grimacing at the leeches. "I need none of those bloodsuckers or tooth pullers. My thanks to you, all the same."

"Another time, then, your worship," said the dapper barber-surgeon, taking Sebastian's arm. "But tell me now, your honor, how did you fare along the roads? Have you just come to Darmstel? An easy journey? On foot, did you say?"

"On my two feet, indeed," Sebastian ruefully replied. "If you could see them, you'd not have to guess. I think I gained three blisters for every half-league."

"Ah?" said the barber, clicking his tongue sympathetically. "You suffer from vesicular bullification. A common complaint."

"I should think so, for anyone who walks the Royal Highway," Sebastian said. "I'd call it a golden road for none but the Regent."

The barber pursed his lips and raised his eyebrows. "Now it's curious your worship comes to that conclusion. Do you say the Regent profits at the expense of his own subjects?"

"So I say, and so does everyone," Sebastian replied. "The Regent has both hands in everybody's pockets. Or around their throats."

The barber sighed. "Yes, your worship, I suppose the times do pinch in Hamelin-Loring."

"Choke, you might say," retorted Sebastian. "Pinch is putting it too gently."

"Well, your worship, you seem a gentleman of spirit—and a gay blade with the ladies, too, your honor, I'll be bound—so you should have no trouble making your way. But where is your way, did you mention?"

"That I don't know," Sebastian answered, "though I wish I did." In spite of his obsequious manner, the barber appeared eager to be friendly; and Sebastian was by no means displeased at being called "your worship" and "your honor" and being taken for a dashing gentleman, after all the insults from the Merry Host and the baker. And so he continued, as a thought suddenly came to him, lowering his voice and saying to the barber:

"When I was on the road, I heard some talk of a Captain

Freeling. He needs good men to follow him, but no one's sure where to find him. Now, surely you're better-traveled than I am, and you might know something of this Captain?"

The barber frowned and shook his head. "Why, your honor, you could likely tell me more than I could tell you. Exactly and precisely what has your worship heard? There's loose tongues in Hamelin-Loring, all ready to wag with no truth whatever. Who was it, in fact, spoke of the Captain? And where? These little details, your honor, might help you sift fact from idle gossip."

Before Sebastian could answer, the innkeeper came up quickly to say that the house was crowded and if he hoped for a bed he would be well advised to find one without delay.

Taking leave of the barber, Sebastian hurried up the stairs, with Presto bounding after. The chamber to which the innkeeper had directed him was already overflowing with travelers. Sebastian went on to the next, opened the door, and peered in. The room was small and stuffy, with half a candle burning in a saucer on the table. A bucket of wash water stood in a corner. As far as Sebastian could see, however, there was only one occupant, stretched out on a straw pallet: a fellow who had gone to bed without having gone to the trouble of undressing.

Pleased by his good luck at finding a single bedmate instead of half a dozen, he stepped inside and called out good-naturedly, "Now, friend, I don't like to disturb your sleeping, since you're doing so well at it; but there's room for another if you'd be so good as to shove yourself over a little."

His bedfellow made no reply beyond burying his head deeper into the bolster.

Sebastian repeated his request. As there was still no answer, he urged:

"Come now, let's have a place there, too. No need to be selfish in the matter of a little straw."

So saying, he sat down on the narrow edge of the pallet and without further ado began to unbutton his jacket, deciding that one way or another he would have a share of the bed, for he was bone-weary after the day's long tramp.

The fellow stirred, and slipped away to the side.

"That's better, and I thank you," Sebastian called over his shoulder, still in the midst of pulling off his jacket. "Share and share alike makes good companions."

An instant later, Sebastian was sitting on the floor, gasping and choking under a flood of cold water, with the bucket on his head.

# How Sebastian Misjudged His Opponent

Sputtering and shouting indignantly, Sebastian flung off the bucket and scrambled to his feet. His jacket, shirt, and breeches were sopping, and water had poured even into his boots. His fellow traveler had meanwhile backed against the wall.

"Is that your notion of a joke?" Sebastian cried. "It's not mine! Come out of that corner and fight like a man!"

In answer, his chamber mate reached out and fetched him a sharp box on the ear.

All the more furious at being so smartly buffeted, in addition to being kept from his bed and soaked to the skin, Sebastian put up his fists. His adversary, with much reluctance, raised his hands defensively but made no move to leave the protection of the corner.

"So, so!" cried Sebastian. "You've played your prank. Now you'll pay for it!"

Just then, the door burst open and Nicholas hurried into the room. Behind him crowded the innkeeper and a handful of guests, some already in their nightcaps, others drawn from the eating room by Sebastian's indignant outcries.

"Gently, gently," commanded Nicholas. "Have done, both of you. There's no quarrel that can't be quietly settled."

By repeated assurances there had been no bloodshed, nor likelihood of any, Nicholas soon succeeded in dispersing the onlookers, among them the barber, who had come with his case under his arm, sniffing out possible business and hopeful that his ministrations would be needed.

Sebastian, during this, had calmed down enough to look closer at his adversary. Instead of a grown man, he saw a lad fully a head shorter than himself, whose long and disheveled black hair tumbled over a pale, frightened face. The boy's jacket was of excellent quality but outrageous fit, for it reached below his knees, nearly as long as his breeches, which had been belted up as far as they would go. The shirt was a fine white lawn, but meant for a stouter wearer, and the youth seemed ready at any moment to disappear into his clothes.

"Well, and what have we here?" exclaimed Sebastian. "A pup? A cub? Now, my lad, you've had a narrow escape. You might have been pounded to a pulp! Let that be a lesson for you, trifling with your elders."

Nicholas stepped closer to the boy, and said in a quiet voice, "No harm will come to you, and surely not from my excitable friend here. But you've run risk enough in traveling alone."

"Yes, and you'd better do as I tell you," put in Sebastian. "I can see at a glance you're a runaway apprentice of one sort or another. So, hurry back to your master."

At this, Nicholas began to chuckle. "An apprentice? I should hardly think so. A runaway? Yes, I should say for certain that she is."

"She?" Sebastian repeated. "She? Nicholas, you've gone out of your wits, taking a baker's boy or printer's devil for a girl."

Nicholas grinned at him. "Had you looked a little closer, you'd have known it from the first. Her jacket's belted wrong side to, for one thing. And is there a boy older than a baby who'd make a fist with his thumb tucked under his fingers?"

Sebastian gaped in astonishment, realizing Nicholas had

spoken the truth. The uncropped hair was indeed too long for a boy's, and the features too smooth and finely drawn.

"Ah—ah, well, of course," Sebastian stammered, reluctant to admit he had been doubly fooled. "I'd have seen it for myself in another moment. It strikes the eye! A runaway goose-girl or kitchenmaid. To think she almost traded blows with me, skinny and scrawny as she is!"

The girl gasped with indignation.

Nicholas clucked his tongue placatingly, and said, "Oh, I doubt if those white hands ever fed geese or scraped pots."

He pursed his lips and shook his head, as though dismayed by his own observation.

"No matter what she is," replied Sebastian, "the Golden Stag's no place for her." He turned to the girl. "Now, missy, tell us what brought you here and you'll have our help in setting matters right."

The girl raised her head and, looking straight at Sebastian, declared in a very earnest and dignified tone:

"Sir, in future and presumably more favorable circumstances, your courtesy shall be both gratefully remembered and appropriately recompensed. Be assured also that the emptying of that receptacle was the result of momentary confusion, and should not be construed as indicating ill intent or deliberate malice. However, since you offer to be of service, your most accommodating and expedient course will be, sir, to depart from these premises."

"What?" Sebastian burst out. "We mean to help you—but if I understand half what you're saying, you're telling us to be off!"

The girl looked calmly at him with cool, deep green eyes.

"If the suggestion is unacceptable," she declared, "the only remaining alternative must be assumed."

So saying, she turned and strode to the door.

Nicholas, with astonishing spryness, hustled ahead of her. Though his brow wrinkled apologetically, and his mild eyes blinked so that he looked like a flustered and embarrassed cherub, he planted himself solidly at the doorway and showed no intention of moving from that spot.

"Now, now, now," he murmured hastily. "A delicate matter, that's true, and likely none of my business at all. But it scrapes my conscience to see any lass alone and undefended. And more so, when the lass happens to be Princess Isabel of Hamelin-Loring."